# SPECIAL CHRISTMAS

"Steve, it's going to be the best Christmas ever!" Elizabeth declared.

"Whoa," Steven said, shaking his head sadly as he looked at the twins. "I just found something out that made my Christmas spirit dry up in a flash."

"What is it?" The twins exchanged anxious glances.

"What would you say if I told you that the Abominable Snowman is coming to stay with us—and there's nothing we can do about it?"

Elizabeth looked completely baffled. "Steve, what are you talking about?"

"Mr. Devlin," Steven said, pronouncing the name as though it hurt to say it, "called from New York just after I got home."

"Go on," Jessica said. "What did he say?"

"He said," Steven continued, "that everything's all set. Suzanne will be arriving Sunday afternoon. And she'll be staying here for two whole weeks!"

"Suzanne Devlin," Elizabeth said, her face draining of color. "But, Steve, that's impossible!"

Bantam Books in the Sweet Valley High Series
Ask your bookseller for the books you have missed

# SWEET VALLEY HIGH
## Super Edition

# SPECIAL CHRISTMAS

Written by
**Kate William**

Created by
**FRANCINE PASCAL**

**BANTAM BOOKS**
TORONTO · NEW YORK · LONDON · SYDNEY · AUCKLAND

RL 6, IL age 12 and up

SPECIAL CHRISTMAS
*A Bantam Book / December 1985*

*Sweet Valley High is a trademark of Francine Pascal*

*Conceived by Francine Pascal*

*Produced by Cloverdale Press, Inc.,
133 Fifth Avenue, New York, N.Y. 10003.*

*Cover art by James Mathewuse*

ISBN 0-553-25377-8

*Published simultaneously in the United States and Canada*

PRINTED IN THE UNITED STATES OF AMERICA

O    0 9 8 7 6 5 4 3 2 1

*To Amy Boesky*

# One

"I give up." Mr. Collins laughed, crossed his arms, and leaned back against his desk. "No one should ever try to teach English the day before Christmas vacation!"

His words met with a burst of applause from the students eagerly eyeing the clock in his classroom. "You tell 'em, Collins!" John Pfeifer, a broad-framed boy, who was sports editor of the Sweet Valley High paper, *The Oracle*, called from the back of the room.

"Take a seat, John," Mr. Collins chided. John was known for his school spirit. That day, however, his spirit was running higher than usual. But Mr. Collins was far too good with students to object to the merriment he was witnessing. Blond, blue-eyed, with little wrinkles around the corners of his eyes that showed when he smiled, Mr. Collins was one of the most popular teachers at Sweet Valley High. Some of the girls insisted he looked like a movie star, but that wasn't the reason why he won the Best-Liked-Teacher award year after year. Mr. Collins was an excellent sport. He knew when to be stern and when to relax. And that day—with a big Christmas party in the gym ready to start any minute—he knew enough not to expect anyone to concentrate on *The Crucible*.

"Ow!" Elizabeth Wakefield cried involuntarily as a wad of paper hit her in the neck. Her blond ponytail fell forward as she leaned over to pick it up. Smoothing out the paper, she saw that a message was scrawled in red Magic Marker. "Liz: Be my Secret Santa," the note read. "Love, John."

Elizabeth bit her lip to keep from laughing out loud. John was absolutely impossible! He knew she was helping Mr. Collins assign Secret Santas at the Christmas party that afternoon, and ever since he'd found out that she'd be matching people up, he'd been bugging her with silly notes. They were good friends, and they both worked on *The Oracle*, so Elizabeth didn't take the notes seriously.

She was glad Mr. Collins had singled her out to help him with the Secret Santa lists. If it weren't for the reporting she'd done for *The Oracle*, for which Mr. Collins was the faculty adviser, she probably wouldn't have gotten the chance. Because she wrote the "Eyes and Ears" column each week as well as some other articles, she had become very close to Mr. Collins.

"Be my Secret Santa," Elizabeth murmured, rereading John's silly note. She smiled. Elizabeth adored Christmas. A holiday atmosphere had gradually pervaded the entire school, making her excitement grow. That afternoon her brother Steven was coming back from college, and the Christmas vacation would start in earnest.

It was going to be the best Christmas ever for Elizabeth and her twin sister, Jessica. They'd been planning it for ages, and Elizabeth was sure everything would go exactly as they'd hoped.

"Liz!" She heard a familiar voice hissing urgently. "Are you dreaming, or what?"

Elizabeth spun around to see her friend, Olivia Davidson smiling at her. Olivia was also on the *Oracle* staff. "You looked so funny. What were you thinking about, staring off into space like that?"

Elizabeth burst out laughing. "Don't tell me the bell rang already," she said, watching her classmates getting up from their desks and frantically getting their things together.

"You weren't in *that* much of a daze," Olivia reassured her. "No, Mr. Collins just said we could all head over to the gym ten minutes early. We're not getting any work done anyway!"

"Olivia," Elizabeth said happily, "don't you just *love* Christmas? I feel like I've got an overdose of Yuletide cheer or something this year."

Olivia's eyes sparkled happily. "I don't suppose," she suggested, dropping her voice, "that has anything to do with a special Christmas visit from someone named Todd Wilkins, does it?"

"It may," Elizabeth said, smiling.

"How many days now?" Olivia pressed as they headed for the door.

"Three," Elizabeth said. It was Friday. Christmas was still ten days away, but Monday Todd was coming back to visit. It had been so long. . . . Elizabeth tried to imagine what it would be like to feel his arms around her, to feel his gentle kiss on her lips.

Elizabeth and Todd had met each other at Sweet Valley High. And they had quickly fallen in love. Todd was such a wonderful guy, she thought, stopping by Olivia's locker and leaning against another locker as she remembered his warm, coffee-brown eyes, his tall basketball-player's build, his thick brown hair . . .

Elizabeth had felt as if her world was collapsing when Todd's father was transferred to Vermont. Vermont. It seemed like the other side of the world! They were both brokenhearted. They had done everything they could to adjust to the move, but distance, they had both discovered, didn't make the heart grow fonder. Long-

4

distance love was hard. It made them both lonesome and sad.

And now Todd was coming back for a visit— for two whole weeks. Elizabeth sighed almost involuntarily. What would it be like? she wondered. How would it *really* feel to see Todd again, after such a long time? She was almost as nervous about seeing Todd as she was excited. What if they'd grown apart? What if the magic wasn't there anymore?

"Elizabeth," a grumpy voice said, less than an inch from her ear. Elizabeth's eyes flew open. "I can't believe it." Jessica moaned and turned to Olivia as if to get some sympathy. "I have some kind of zombie for a twin. She stands around in the hall with a dumb expression on her face all day!"

"Jess," Elizabeth cried, throwing both arms around her twin. "It's almost Christmas!"

"I know, I know." Jessica giggled and tried to disentangle herself. "How long has she *been* like this?" she asked Olivia, her aqua eyes sparkling.

The Wakefields looked at each other, conspiratorial grins spreading across their faces. There was nothing they loved better than teamwork.

It was easy to see why. A passing stranger would have stopped in his tracks, thinking his eyes were playing tricks on him, because the two girls looked exactly alike. They were both slender and five-foot-six-inches tall. They both had sun-streaked blond hair that cascaded gently to their shoulders, and wide-set, blue-green eyes fringed with long lashes.

Usually the twins dressed very differently. Elizabeth preferred classic, tailored clothes, and Jessica liked whatever was in the latest issue of her favorite fashion magazines. But that day they were wearing matching outfits—navy cotton skirts and light blue short-sleeved sweaters that showed off their tans perfectly. Even the gold lavalieres dangling from their necks were identical—presents from their parents on their sixteenth birthday.

"Hey, you two," Olivia said. "What's with your outfits? You're not planning something, are you?" she added, her eyes narrowing.

Elizabeth burst out laughing, and Jessica joined in.

"Of course not," Jessica scoffed. She and Elizabeth had been known to trick people in the past, but only when they were really in trouble. That is, only when *Jessica* was really in trouble. For despite their appearance, Jessica was as different from Elizabeth as night from day. Elizabeth was the more serious twin, always volunteering for things and joining committees and working on her writing. Even *boys* were serious as far as Elizabeth was concerned—a concept Jessica found hard to imagine. She couldn't believe Elizabeth would want to keep up a relationship for so long—especially when Todd was away in Vermont. Sure Todd was good-looking and everything—Jessica wouldn't deny *that*. But Elizabeth was so earnest!

Jessica liked things to be fun. *Fun* was her philosophy for everything, from cheerleading to parties to afternoons at the beach. If something wasn't fun, she didn't want any part of it. And if it *was* fun, it was worth taking a risk for. That meant she got into scrapes from time to time. But she'd always gotten out of them in the end—with Elizabeth's help and lots of luck.

"Why else would you two dress like carbon copies?" Olivia demanded. "You've got to be up to *something*."

"You tell her," Jessica said, her eyes lighting up as she caught sight of a tall, blond boy on the other side of the hall. "I've got to run. I'll see you two at the party."

"Looks like Jess is on the prowl." Elizabeth laughed. "Isn't that the exchange student who just arrived from Germany?"

Olivia nodded. "His name is Hans. He's trying to improve his English. But even with a language barrier, your twin never seems to have trouble," she commented wryly.

Elizabeth smiled. She worried about Jessica from time to time, but she adored her sister and wouldn't let anything in the world come between them. And she knew Jessica felt exactly the same way about her. "We're having our picture taken together at Hunt's Photography this afternoon," she confided as the two headed for

7

the gym. "It's going to be our Christmas present for our parents this year. We thought it would be fun to dress alike. Mom and Dad had a portrait done of us when we were little girls, and we were wearing navy skirts and white blouses. So we thought we'd dress the same way for this picture."

"Your parents will love it."

"I hope so." Elizabeth laughed. "It was hard to convince Jess to come to school dressed so simply—especially on the day of the Christmas party!"

"Liz!" Mr. Collins called, hurrying over to greet the girls as they entered the crowded gym. "I need your help on the Secret Santa assignments. It looks like the natives are getting restless!"

Secret Santa was an important part of Christmastime at Sweet Valley High. Every student in the school was given another student's name on a slip of paper. The idea was to be a Santa for the person whose name you were given—to buy presents or do special things for that person while keeping your identity a secret. At the same time someone *else* was being a Secret Santa for you. This went on for an entire week, until the Christmas dance, when all Santas revealed their identities at the stroke of midnight.

Elizabeth was convinced this year Secret Santa Week would be better than ever. For one thing, Bruce Patman had offered to have the Christmas dance up at the Patmans' mansion. The Patmans were one of the richest families in town, and their parties were always memorable.

Elizabeth took a seat beside Mr. Collins at the table in one corner of the gym.

"OK," Mr. Collins told her. "All you do is pass the basket with the names in it to each person who comes up. Then make a mark next to the name on the computer printout and move on. Easy as pie!"

"I barely recognize this place," Elizabeth told him, looking across the gym. A huge tree was set up at one end of the room. Boughs of evergreen and holly were everywhere. Green and red streamers festooned and bleachers and basketball hoops, and tables set up with luscious-looking food lined both sides of the room. The band was playing Christmas carols, and general chaos seemed to be reigning as the entire student body poured in through the doors.

"I appreciate your help," Mr. Collins told Elizabeth as the first crush of students approached the table. "I know it isn't much of a party for you this way."

"It's wonderful," Elizabeth assured him. "I'm glad to help out." The truth was that Elizabeth had the ideal vantage point for observing. Everyone had to get a Secret Santa assignment, so she was able to say hello to her friends: Aaron Dallas, the tall, good-looking captain of the soccer team; Roger Barrett Patman, Bruce's cousin;

9

his girlfriend Olivia Davidson; Caroline Pearce, a redhead for whom Elizabeth felt a special fondness after having helped her through a difficult time.

Just then Cara Walker—a sleek brunette who was one of Jessica's closest friends—came to the table alone, asking if Elizabeth had seen Jessica anywhere. Elizabeth had been looking for her twin for a while. She wanted to set up a meeting place so they could leave for the photographer's together. But even Lila Fowler—one of the richest girls in school, and Jessica's dear friend and arch-rival combined—hadn't seen her.

At last Jessica appeared, looking uncharacteristically conservative in her navy skirt and blue sweater. Hans, the foreign-exchange student, was by her side. "Hans needs a Secret Santa," Jessica said pointedly. The look she gave Elizabeth clearly meant: *Make sure you give him my name.* But there was nothing Elizabeth could do, even if she wanted to cheat. The names were in a basket, and all she could do was to pass the whole lot to Hans and wish for the best.

"Who is this?" Hans asked Elizabeth in his thick accent after Jessica had walked away.

Elizabeth looked at the piece of paper and sighed, "Lila Fowler," she told him, pointing out the brown-haired, attractive girl on the other side of the gym. "Don't tell anyone," she warned him. "It has to be a secret." *Jessica*, she thought, *is going to be fit to be tied if she finds out before next Friday.*

It was obvious that Jessica had a crush on Hans. And she was hardly going to be thrilled if she discovered he was rushing around getting presents for Lila Fowler!

"Hey, Liz!" Ken Matthews called, hurrying to the table. Captain of the football team, Ken was a friendly, outgoing guy with broad shoulders, and blond good looks. "Don't tell me," Ken said, shooting a glance at Mr. Collins to make sure he was busy with the computer printout of student names and wasn't listening. "Just keeping yourself busy till the old flame gets back in town, huh?"

Todd was going to be staying with Ken and he had been teasing Elizabeth about Todd's arrival for the last few days.

She decided to ignore his comment. "Just choose your Secret Santa, Ken," she advised, holding out the basket filled with names.

Ken grinned. "Guess you won't need one of those," he said slyly, taking a slip of paper and scanning the name briefly before folding it up and slipping it in his pocket. "Todd Wilkins will be all the Secret Santa you can handle."

*I hope so,* Elizabeth thought. A few months ago, Todd's visit would have been the best Christmas present Elizabeth could have hoped for. Now her feelings were scrambled. She just

11

didn't know *how* she felt. And it looked as if she'd have to wait till Monday to find out.

"Vacation!" Jessica shrieked, throwing her book bag in the air and catching it with both arms. "Liz, we're on *vacation*—nothing but Secret Santas and buying presents and the parade and Bruce's fabulous, fabulous Christmas dance—"

"And picking up Mom and Dad's present a week from today," Elizabeth reminded her, running her turquoise eyes over the bill the photographer had presented her at the door.

The twins were in the parking lot of Hunt's Photography, having just finished their photo session with Mr. Hunt himself. He had promised a beautiful picture—enlarged and framed by the following week, ready to slip under the tree.

"Do you think it'll really be OK?" Elizabeth asked, opening the door to the red Fiat Spider the twins shared, and slipping into the driver's seat.

Jessica bounded around to the other side of the sleek little convertible. "Don't be such a worrier," she said lightly. "It's a perfect present for Mom and Dad. They'll love it!"

Elizabeth wished she had Jessica's confidence that a reproduction of their image would be the best gift imaginable. "I hope you're right," Elizabeth said as she started up the engine.

But Jessica didn't respond. She was a million miles away. "Isn't Hans gorgeous?" she asked a minute or two later as her twin edged the Fiat out onto the street.

"He's OK," Elizabeth said noncommittally. Jessica's thoughts were on Hans, and hers were on Todd. They drove in silence for a few minutes, and then Elizabeth said, "I can't imagine Christmas in a cold climate. Poor Todd—stuck up north with all that snow!"

Jessica snorted. "He'll be back in the land of sunshine and Elizabeth Wakefield soon enough," she pointed out. "But I do know what you mean," she added a moment later. "I love Christmastime in Sweet Valley. It's so much fun to swim in the pool on Christmas Eve. And I guess the warm weather forces people to use their imaginations. Remember what the Fowlers did last year to decorate their house?"

Elizabeth groaned, then laughed. Lila's father's computer company had made him a wealthy man practically overnight. Sometimes he went overboard trying to show what he could afford. The previous year he had spent a fortune having a "winter wonderland" set up on the rolling lawn in front of the Fowlers' mansion. The display featured a sleigh with eight plastic reindeer and a life-size Santa, false ice statues, and artificial snowmen. "It was the tackiest thing ever," Jessica remembered happily.

Elizabeth shot her a knowing look. "How are

13

things with Lila these days?" she asked. Jessica and Lila were just about due for a huge fight, judging from the peace and quiet they'd been experiencing for weeks.

"She's being a real pain," Jessica said shortly.

Elizabeth's eyebrows shot up. "What's up this time?"

Jessica groaned. "She wants to be Miss Christmastime this year and ride on the first float in the parade. I can't stand it! She knows how badly I want that title. I was runner-up last year, and if it weren't for Lila deciding at the last minute she wants it, I *know* I could win."

Elizabeth sighed. So that was it. The annual Christmas parade was a big deal in Sweet Valley. It took place every year at the same time—the day before Christmas. Miss Christmastime was usually chosen a week before. She wore a silver crown and a gorgeous dress, and waved to the spectators from the lavish float at the head of the parade. Personally Elizabeth couldn't imagine anything worse than smiling and waving for hours, but she could see how badly Jessica wanted to win. "I wouldn't worry," Elizabeth said. "If *I* were a judge, I'd choose you over Lila any day!"

"Well, the decision will be made tomorrow," Jessica told her. "I have to be at the civic center tomorrow afternoon at three-thirty. The judges ask us all a bunch of questions, and there's a short runway competition. And then we'll know."

The twins had reached the Wakefields' driveway, and Elizabeth felt a surge of relief as she parked the Fiat in front of the attractive, split-level home where they lived. It was Christmas vacation—honest and truly, Christmas vacation. Now she could relax, catch up on everything with Steven—and wait for Monday.

"Hey," Jessica said suddenly, getting out of the car, "you never told me who you got for Secret Santa."

"That's why it's called secret!" She had drawn Aaron Dallas's name out of the hat, but she didn't see why she should tell her twin about it.

"I got someone impossible," Jessica told her. "Absolutely impossible. It's—"

"Jess!" Elizabeth wailed. "Don't *tell* me. You're not supposed to—"

"Bruce," Jessica continued. "Bruce Patman. What in the world do you give to a guy who already has everything?" Jessica sighed as the girls walked in the house together.

"It depends," a deep voice answered. "How about a Christmas hug?"

"Steve!" the twins cried in unison, throwing their arms around their brother.

"When did you get home?" Elizabeth asked, stepping back to look her brother over from head to foot. He looked terrific, as usual. With his dark brown hair, brown eyes; and athletic build, he was the image of Mr. Wakefield at eighteen.

"About an hour ago," Steven told her, disentangling himself from Jessica's exuberant embrace.

"We're so *excited*," Jessica shrieked. "I'm going to win the Miss Christmastime title, and we've got Secret Santas, and, Steve, there's a wonderful Christmas dance you have to come to a week from tonight, it's up at the Patmans', and—"

"We're all together!" Elizabeth broke in, unable to stay calm a minute longer. "Steve, it's going to be the best Christmas ever!"

"Whoa," Steven said, stepping back and shaking his head sadly as he looked from one radiant face to the other. "I hate to sound like Scrooge, you two, but I just found something out that made my Christmas spirit dry up just like that." Steven snapped his finger, his face darkening.

"What is it?" the twins demanded, exchanging anxious glances.

"What would you say," Steven began slowly, taking a deep breath, "if I told you that the Abominable Snowman is coming to spend two whole weeks with us—and there's nothing we can do about it?"

"The Abominable Snowman," Elizabeth repeated, completely baffled. "Steve, what on earth are you talking about?"

"Mr. Devlin," Steven said, pronouncing the

16

name as though it hurt his mouth to say it, "called from New York just after I got home. He wanted to speak to Mom or Dad, and I told him they were both at work."

"Go on," Jessica said. "What did he say, Steve?"

"He said," Steven continued, "that everything's all set, the plans made just the way they discussed them. Suzanne will be arriving Sunday afternoon on the one o'clock flight from New York City. And she'll be staying here for two whole weeks!"

"Suzanne Devlin," Elizabeth said, her face draining of color. "But, Steve, that's impossible!"

"That's what I thought," Steven said flatly. "But Mom called from work about five minutes ago, and I gave her the message. I said I couldn't believe it was true. She sounded really funny. She told me that we'd talk about it at dinner—and she wouldn't say anything else."

"Then it *must* be true!" Jessica shrieked, looking anguished. "How in the world can Mom and Dad ruin our vacation by inviting that horrible creep to stay here with us—after what she did to Liz the last time she was here!"

Nobody said a word. Elizabeth was too horrified to speak, and from the look on Steven's face, it seemed as though he shared her feelings.

The best Christmas ever was ruined.

And it was all Suzanne Devlin's fault—again!

# Two

Elizabeth was lying on her bed upstairs, her head in her hands. *How can Mom and Dad do this to us?* she wondered, shaking her head in disbelief. Suzanne Devlin . . .

"It can't be happening," Elizabeth repeated for almost the hundredth time. "It just can't be! This is a bad dream, and any minute I'll wake up and laugh at myself for having believed anything this rotten could happen."

But Elizabeth knew she wasn't dreaming. And until her parents got home from work, all she could do was wait with the questions she had.

Wait, and remember.

Suzanne Devlin was sixteen years old, the same age as the twins. All their lives the twins had heard their father talk about Tom Devlin, and they'd always looked forward to meeting him—and especially to meeting his daughter.

Tom Devlin had gone to college with Mr. Wakefield, and they had remained friends over the years, although they lived in different cities and had pursued very different careers. Ned Wakefield was a successful and hard-working attorney, deeply dedicated to the law—but as he often told the twins, his family came first to him. Mr. Devlin had always sounded terribly glamorous to the twins. He was a diplomat, and he had lived in no less than sixteen countries since he and Mr. Wakefield had left college. Sixteen countries! The twins thought that sounded wonderful. Suzanne was the Devlins' only child. They had tried to take her with them as often as possible, and when they couldn't, they had sent her to boarding schools. She'd even been to school in Switzerland!

For the past few years, the Devlins' permanent home had been a luxurious apartment on Park Avenue in New York City. The twins had almost gone out of their minds when Mr. Wakefield told them that the Devlins had suggested a daughter exchange for the week of spring vacation. They'd both wanted to go to New York so badly that in the end they flipped a coin to decide. Elizabeth had won.

Elizabeth shook her head now and smiled, remembering the anguish on Jessica's face when she realized she'd lost. Jessica had been impos-

20

sible. She'd even started hinting that Lila had a crush on Todd and if Elizabeth went away, it would be only a matter of days before she lost her boyfriend. When Jessica wanted something, it was hard not to give in to her. And Elizabeth hadn't cared that much. She wasn't really a big-city person, and after some strong persuasive tactics on Jessica's part, she'd agreed to stay in Sweet Valley and send her twin off to Manhattan.

At first Elizabeth was overjoyed by the way things had turned out. Suzanne Devlin had impressed everyone as being a perfect angel. If Elizabeth had been slightly concerned that a sophisticated New Yorker would be bored in Sweet Valley, her fears were melted by Suzanne's manner. Everything was *darling* to Suzanne. She *loved* Sweet Valley. She thought everyone she met was *charming*, and she was simply knocked out by the Wakefields' *adorable* house.

If anything, Elizabeth had had to pinch herself to prove Suzanne wasn't a dream. She seemed almost too good to be true. In the first place, she was unusually beautiful. About an inch taller than the twins, she had long, silky, raven-black hair that fell in shimmering waves past her shoulders. And her complexion! Her skin was luminous. She had wide-set eyes that were an incredible blue-violet color. And her *clothes* . . .

It was like having a fashion model visit! Wher-

ever they went—even if it was just to a picnic—
Suzanne looked as though she'd gone shopping
ten minutes before and selected the ideal outfit.

With looks like that—and with a strong dose of
charm—Suzanne was a big hit with the guys she
met. Aaron Dallas, in particular, was attracted to
her. And so was poor Winston Egbert.

Elizabeth couldn't fault Aaron or Winston for
being enthralled by Suzanne. Elizabeth had been
more charmed than anyone. How could she help
it? She'd been nervous about meeting this big-
city girl, and Suzanne couldn't have been
friendlier. Or more helpful. She jumped up to do
the dishes every night after dinner. She thanked
the Wakefields constantly for everything; she
was fascinated by everything Elizabeth did, and
all Elizabeth's friends struck her as so wonderful
that she made a special effort to get to know
them all better.

*I was such a fool*, Elizabeth remembered. *I really
fell for it*.

The first hint that something was wrong came
on the day Elizabeth's gold lavaliere was missing. That necklace meant the world to her. She
always took special care to leave it on her dresser
at night so it wouldn't get tangled when she
slept. She had gone crazy when she couldn't find
the necklace. She'd looked everywhere for it.
And Suzanne had searched, too.

Or so she'd said.

Then there had been the horrible incident with

Mr. Collins. *That* was the worst thing Suzanne had done, and Elizabeth would never forgive her for it. Never!

Suzanne had liked Mr. Collins from the day she met him. *Everyone* liked Mr. Collins, and Elizabeth didn't think anything of it. But Suzanne had more than the ordinary kind of affection in mind. She did everything she could to get Mr. Collins to pay attention to her. She even faked drowning at a class picnic so he'd swim out and rescue her! Again, at the time Elizabeth had thought nothing of it. She'd forgotten that Suzanne was an excellent swimmer. How could she suspect someone who was so charming, so kind, of having ulterior motives? As everyone else, Elizabeth had believed the incident was an accident.

Then one night Suzanne persuaded Elizabeth to let her baby-sit in Elizabeth's place for Teddy Collins, Mr. Collins's adorable six-year-old son. Elizabeth knew she shouldn't let Suzanne fill in for her without consulting Mr. Collins first, but Suzanne seemed so trustworthy, so responsible.

That night was the beginning of one of the worst times ever for Elizabeth. Suzanne came home in hysterics, her blouse torn and her hair unkempt. She told Elizabeth and the Wakefields that Mr. Collins had forced himself on her, started kissing her, trying all sorts of things. . . . It was horrible. Mr. Collins? No one would have believed it. But one look at Suzanne, and what else could they think? She was the last person they'd suspect of lying.

Within days the whole community was involved in the Collins scandal. It looked as if the most popular teacher at Sweet Valley High was going to lose his job. Deep down Elizabeth didn't know what to believe. She'd known Mr. Collins for years and had always trusted him. Was it possible he could have done such a thing?

Now Elizabeth felt like kicking herself for having been so gullible. But it hadn't been just her. Everyone had been taken in.

Suzanne was a marvelous actress. When she wanted to be charming, she could pour it on. If it hadn't been for Winston, no one ever would have found out the truth.

But Elizabeth had gone to Lila's birthday party with a good idea that Suzanne Devlin had a few things to explain. Suzanne was leaving the next day, and Elizabeth had decided to place a surprise present in the girl's half-packed suitcase. It was then that Elizabeth had come across her necklace.

If Suzanne had lied about her necklace, Elizabeth had reasoned, wasn't it possible she was lying about Mr. Collins, too?

At Lila Fowler's party that night Suzanne was in top form, as usual. Aaron Dallas was doing his best to keep her happy, bringing her drinks and laughing at every joke she made. But it was obvious that Suzanne's act was wearing thin. When

Winston Egbert overheard the argument between Elizabeth and Suzanne over the stolen necklace, he decided it was time to expose Suzanne's true nature.

Suzanne was dancing with Aaron Dallas, and Winston walked over to them, carrying a full glass of punch. He pretended to trip and spilled the ruby-colored liquid all over Suzanne's white dress. Her facade crumbled. She flew into a tantrum, screaming terrible things at him. Everyone was amazed. Was *this* the wonderful, considerate, devoted guest they'd been trying so hard to entertain?

Elizabeth's head throbbed as she remembered the events of that evening. It had all come out then—how hurt Suzanne had been that Mr. Collins treated her like a child and how glad she'd been to get back at him. He hadn't attacked her at all. If anything, it was the other way around.

It made Elizabeth sick to think about it. *I hate her*, she thought furiously, sitting up and brushing her hair from her face. *I absolutely hate her!*

Elizabeth had never felt so strongly about anyone. She wasn't used to disliking people. But what Suzanne had tried to do to Mr. Collins was horrible, and it was dishonest. And Elizabeth hated dishonesty.

*Besides*, she reminded herself, *she wasn't just dishonest to poor Mr. Collins. She was deceiving all of us—trying to act sweet and helpful when secretly she thought we were a bunch of idiots.*

*And she was dishonest to me. Not just trying to steal my necklace—that was bad enough. But winning me over, making me like her and care about her. And then making a fool of me!*

For the life of her, Elizabeth couldn't imagine why her parents would agree to let Suzanne come back. *And without even asking us!* Elizabeth thought. It wasn't like her parents—not one tiny bit. What in the world, Elizabeth wondered, could have made them do something like this to us?

And particularly smack in the middle of the most magical holiday of the whole year!

As if her twin had been reading her mind, Elizabeth's bedroom door flew open, and Jessica rushed in, obviously agitated.

"We're not going to take this lying down," Jessica declared, hurling herself onto Elizabeth's bed.

"You sound like you're on the set of a western or something," Elizabeth said gloomily. "What are we supposed to do, Jess? Lock ourselves in our rooms for the whole Christmas holiday?"

"Jess is right," Steven said, coming into the room and sinking down into a chair in the corner by the window. "We've got to do something. Fast!"

Elizabeth shook her head, her blond ponytail bobbing emphatically. "No way," she told them. "You two didn't spend any time with Demolition Devlin, remember? And, Jess, you didn't even

26

*meet* her. There's nothing we can do," she concluded tragically, "but just admit it: Christmas vacation is ruined. One hundred percent, completely, totally *ruined*." Steve had been very busy with a personal problem when Suzanne came. And Jessica had been in New York. Elizabeth had told them both every detail about Suzanne, but they still hadn't witnessed any of her treachery firsthand.

"Wait a minute," Jessica said, indignant. "Don't make it sound like *I* didn't suffer, too, Liz. Remember, I was stuck in that morgue of an apartment in New York City. Besides, I got stuck with Suzanne's friends. And believe me, they were worse than Suzanne could be any day! I mean, if she's one bit like them she must be *dreadful*. That girl who'd just spent half her trust fund having plastic surgery on her chin . . ."

"Look," Steven said reasonably. "You two are assuming that all we can do is wait for Suzanne to descend on us and then put up with her. Right?"

The twins turned to stare at him. "What else?" Elizabeth demanded. "We can't *all* send ourselves to the Devlins for the holiday, can we?"

"Why don't we talk to Mom and Dad tonight and tell them how we feel?" Steven suggested. "They're reasonable people, and it seems to me they must have just gone temporarily mad, telling Suzanne she could come back!"

"Maybe Mr. Devlin pressured Daddy into it,"

Jessica said thoughtfully. "There was a movie on TV about that last week. This guy kept leaning on the local drugstore owner, and it turned out it was blackmail. Do you think Daddy—"

"Jess," Elizabeth interrupted. "Mr. Devlin isn't blackmailing anybody. Mom and Dad are probably just too polite to tell them the truth. How do you tell your old friend from college that his daughter is a total creep?"

"I'll do it," Jessica volunteered. "Boy," she added, "after what her *boyfriend* did, I'd be glad to tell her parents!"

"What exactly did her boyfriend do?" Steven asked, looking interested.

Jessica blushed. "Oh, you know," she said, waving her hand dismissively. "He was a complete jerk."

Elizabeth gave her a sympathetic smile. From what Jessica had finally told her about her date with Suzanne's boyfriend Pete, it sounded as though Jessica had been lucky to end the evening the way she had. Used to being able to handle the guys she knew, Jessica had flirted outrageously with Pete. And he had finally responded—but not exactly the way Jessica had planned. He had practically attacked her, and if the Devlins hadn't come home when they had . . .

"The way I see it," Steven was saying, "from everything you two have told me, Suzanne is impossible. Just impossible. We've all got a lot of

28

plans for the holidays, and we've been looking forward to the vacation. We can't let this girl come here and ruin the whole thing!"

"Then what," Elizabeth asked, "are we supposed to do?"

"Yeah, Steve," Jessica echoed, turning to her brother with an imploring look. "You're the one who's in college. You've got to think of a way to save us!"

"I still think talking to Mom and Dad is the best way to go," Steven told them. "We're doing exactly what Dad always says we do—jumping to all sorts of conclusions. Maybe there's a logical explanation for everything. Maybe—"

"Logical explanation, hah!" Jessica snorted. "Besides, we *aren't* jumping to conclusions. Unless that call was a prank, Suzanne is showing up here on Sunday for two dreadful weeks."

"It wasn't a prank." Steven sighed. "Mom made that clear when she called."

"Some help you are," Jessica said. "See what a college education gets you?"

"No, Jess," Elizabeth said, sitting up straighter on her bed. "I think Steve has a good point. Mom and Dad are always saying how important it is to talk things out as a family. And it looks like this is something that really *does* need to be talked about."

"That's right," Steven said. "Maybe Mom and Dad just don't realize how strongly we feel about

Suzanne's coming here. Once we make them realize that—"

"They've flipped," Jessica said stonily. "They've gone completely nuts. No decent parents in their right minds would inflict this kind of torture on their children. It's—it's inhumane!" she concluded lamely, her aqua eyes filling with tears.

"OK, OK," Elizabeth said, hugging her sister and shooting a look at Steve. "Listen, Jess. You know how much Mom and Dad hate it when any of us makes a scene. We've got to be really calm when we talk about this. We have to make them see how reasonable we are and how *un*reasonable it would be to let Suzanne stay here. Do you know what I'm saying?"

"Are you saying I shouldn't be honest about my feelings with my own parents?" Jessica asked.

Elizabeth and Steven exchanged uneasy glances. "No, Jess," Elizabeth began, "that isn't it at all. It's just—"

"Good!" Jessica declared, bouncing off the bed and racing for the door. "Because I'm furious about this whole thing. Daddy always says we should be up front about our feelings, and that's exactly what I'm going to be as soon as he and Mom get home. Completely, devastatingly honest!"

"Oh, boy." Steven sighed as Jessica stormed

out of the room. "I have a feeling it's going to be hard to keep things reasonable after all."

"Steve," Elizabeth said, "I have a feeling you're absolutely right."

# Three

"Now listen to me for just one second," Mr. Wakefield said firmly, leaning back in his chair and loosening his tie. "Jessica, don't you even want to hear our side of the story—your mother's and mine?"

The Wakefields were sitting at their favorite booth at Guido's, the best pizza parlor in town. Mr. Wakefield had worked late, and he'd called home to ask the twins and Steven to meet him and Mrs. Wakefield downtown for dinner. "It'll be fun," he'd said. "We all need to celebrate you two are done with school, Steve's home, and it looks like I'm done with a case I've been working on for some time."

Elizabeth was glad they were eating dinner out. She had a feeling that might diffuse the ten-

33

sion that had built up, since none of the Wake-fields liked family arguments in public places.

Guido's Pizza Palace was a wonderful restau-rant. The Wakefields had been going there for years, and Frank DeLuna, the round-faced, incredibly funny Italian man who managed the place, said Jessica and Elizabeth were his favorite clients.

Alice Wakefield took a sip of her water, then slipped out of her slate-blue suit jacket. "Thank heavens for holidays," she remarked. "You'd think people would get sick and tired of rede-signing their houses, but it never seems to stop!"

Elizabeth glanced admiringly at her mother. Slender and blond, she was often teased about how young she looked. "Like one of these girls," Frank had said that evening, pointing at Jessica and Elizabeth. Mrs. Wakefield had a seemingly endless supply of good sense and professional energy. She was known as one of the top interior designers in the area.

"OK," she said at last, looking soberly around the table. "Now, I suppose you guys want to know why we're letting Suzanne visit for the next two weeks, right?"

"You didn't even *ask* us," Jessica said, injured.

"Jess," Mr. Wakefield said warningly, "we didn't have a chance to, or we would have. Tom Devlin called me last week and said his daughter wanted to get in touch with us. He said she'd been through a great deal recently, and he thought it would mean a lot to her if she could wish us a Merry Christmas, or something. Well, we thought at first all she wanted was to talk on the phone."

"She did call us," Alice Wakefield cut in. "And, as always, she sounded like a sweet, polite young lady. She said she wanted to see us in person, to make it up to us all for having behaved so terribly."

"I don't buy it," Steven said flatly, looking up and thanking the waiter who was setting drinks down all around. "What sort of ordeal could she have gone through? And why would she need to come all the way out here to make it up to all of us? It all sounds kind of fishy to me."

"It sounds *more* than fishy to me," Jessica interrupted.

Mr. and Mrs. Wakefield exchanged glances.

"Look," Mr. Wakefield said, "we feel terrible about imposing Suzanne on you three. But I'm afraid there isn't much we can do about it. Suzanne is intent on coming out here. She's been through a lot, and she wants to prove to you all that she's changed. Don't you feel that she deserves a second chance?"

There was dead silence around the table as the twins and Steven stared at one another.

"Dad," Elizabeth began tentatively, "Suzanne did a lot of damage when she was here before. Maybe we sound like we're being selfish, but it really isn't just *us* we're thinking about. There's

35

Aaron Dallas, for example. And poor Winston Egbert. They liked her so much, and she was awful to them. And Mr. Collins.''

Mrs. Wakefield sighed. ''Suzanne knows that. She's already written to Mr. Collins—and he supports her coming out here. Believe me, Liz, we've been over this again and again. That's why we didn't say anything to you about it at first. We thought we could persuade Suzanne not to come. But I'm afraid she's made up her mind. And your father and I are not the sort of people to deny *anyone* a welcome in our home. We hope you three aren't, either.''

''The pizza's here,'' Mr. Wakefield said, obviously hoping to lighten the tension that had settled over the table.

''It looks wonderful,'' Elizabeth said, smiling sympathetically at her father. It wasn't her parents' fault, she thought. As usual they were just trying to be as thoughtful and considerate as possible. It was Suzanne . . .

''Where are the Devlins going to be over the holidays?'' Jessica asked, reaching for a thick wedge of Guido's deluxe pizza.

Mr. Wakefield set down his glass. ''Saint-Moritz,'' he said quietly. ''You know where that is, don't you?''

''Switzerland,'' Jessica said through a mouthful of pizza. ''Lila's father goes there all the time. It's a really ritzy ski resort, right?''

Mr. Wakefield nodded. ''And Suzanne,'' he

added firmly, "doesn't want to go. She wants to come out here."

"You mean she's only coming out here so she doesn't have to go to Europe?" Elizabeth demanded.

"Your father didn't say that," Mrs. Wakefield corrected gently. "For whatever reason, she wants to come out here. And your father and I are asking you to give her another chance. For our sake as well as hers."

Elizabeth blinked. Give Suzanne another chance?

If it were anyone else—maybe. But not Suzanne. If they gave Suzanne another chance, she'd probably destroy the world.

"I think it's awful," Jessica said miserably, pulling loose a slice of pepperoni and popping it into her mouth.

"You think," Mr. Wakefield repeated, *"what's* awful?"

"The whole thing!" Jessica cried. "Dad, the girl's horrible! She's a thief and a liar and God knows what else. What kind of Christmas are any of us going to have with her on the loose?"

The whole table was quiet for a minute before Mrs. Wakefield spoke. "Jess," she said softly. "Remember what Christmas is all about? This is supposed to be the time of year when you extend goodwill to people who need it. And your father and I both think Suzanne Devlin is one of those people."

"Suzanne Devlin," Jessica said gloomily, "doesn't exactly need goodwill. What Suzanne needs is a good swift kick in the—"

"Aha!" Mr. Wakefield interrupted loudly, ignoring the look on Jessica's face. "Just what the lawyer ordered—another piece of pizza!"

Elizabeth stared down at the table, trying not to let her unhappiness show on her face. Her parents might be right, she thought, swallowing in an attempt to make the lump in her throat go down. This *was* Christmastime, after all, and people were supposed to be more generous and loving than at any other time of the year. It sounded as if Mr. Collins had forgiven her—which was just like him.

But Elizabeth couldn't help feeling he and her parents were sadly mistaken if they really believed Suzanne was coming out to Sweet Valley to make up, to say she was sorry.

No, the one thing Elizabeth had learned—the hard way—was that Suzanne didn't do *anything* unless there was something in it for her.

Elizabeth didn't know what Suzanne could possibly want in Sweet Valley this time.

But unless she, Jessica and Steven could devise a good way to stop her, Elizabeth had a feeling it wouldn't be long before they all found out.

\*    \*    \*

38

Later that evening the twins and Steven sat in Steven's bedroom discussing the situation.

"We've got to think of something," Jessica muttered. "We've just got to!"

"Aren't you supposed to be getting your beauty sleep? I thought the selection for Miss Christmastime was tomorrow afternoon."

Jessica sighed. "The beauty sleep will have to wait. If that Devlin monster is around for the next two weeks, I'm going to get gray hair just from anxiety."

"Jessica's right," Steven said. "I hoped Mom and Dad would be reasonable—but they seem to have gone off the deep end. We're just going to have to take matters into our own hands."

"Liz!" Jessica shrieked, grabbing her sister's hand. "I've got a wonderful, wonderful idea!"

"She means terrible," Elizabeth told Steven. "Meet my twin sister, the Grinch."

"I'm serious!" Jessica gasped. "Where are Mom and Dad?" she demanded, jumping up to close the door to Steven's bedroom.

"Downstairs," Elizabeth told her. "Why?"

"I've really got a good idea. I can't believe we didn't think of it ages ago! Liz, can you sneak downstairs and get the Devlins' phone number?"

"Why?" Elizabeth demanded.

"Trust me," Jessica said. "Dad keeps his address book in the desk in the study."

"I'll get it," Steven said. "But don't start

39

explaining your devious plan until I'm back upstairs, OK?''

Steven returned a few minutes later. "Now, look," Jessica began. "Suzanne may have gone nuts herself, for all we know, but more likely she just wants to come here so she won't have to go to Saint-Moritz, which means she's *really* nuts, but forget that for a minute. Liz, all you have to do is call her up and make her realize how horrible it'll be for her if she comes. And I mean *horrible*. You can sort of drop little hints to let her know that everyone here still hates her and hasn't forgotten any of the awful things she did. She'll never want to come once you've made that clear! I bet she'll *beg* her parents to take her to Saint-Moritz by the time you're through.''

"I don't know," Elizabeth said doubtfully. "You really think that'll work?"

"It just might," Steven said. "Jess is right, Liz. If you really lay it on thick, you might be able to convince her!''

"Well," Elizabeth said uncertainly, "I don't know, you guys. If that's the best we can come up with . . .''

The next thing she knew, Jessica and Steven had pounced on her. "Tickle her!" Jessica yelled. "Tickle her until she promises!''

"Stop it!" Elizabeth gasped, laughing so hard her sides ached. "Come on, you guys, cut it out!''

"Do you promise?" Jessica demanded.

"I promise." Elizabeth moaned. She'd laughed so hard that tears streamed from her eyes. "But I doubt this is going to work," she warned them once they'd stopped torturing her.

"Give it the old college try," Steven urged her. "Come on, Liz. We're counting on you!"

"You're all that stands between us and disaster!" Jessica chimed in.

"I'm calling from my room," Elizabeth said, standing, "or you guys are going to make me crack up."

"Call collect!" Jessica shouted as Elizabeth opened the door.

Elizabeth didn't feel good about what she was about to do. But she couldn't think of a better plan herself. And they had to stop Suzanne from coming. They just had to!"

"Suzanne? It's Elizabeth. Elizabeth Wakefield," Elizabeth said several minutes later, her bedroom door tightly closed.

"Liz!" Suzanne shrieked. "I'm so glad you called!"

"You are?" Elizabeth asked dumbly. "I mean, how are you?" she asked quickly.

"I'm fine," Suzanne said dismissively. "But how are *you*, Liz? It's been so long since we've talked to each other!"

*Not long enough for me*, Elizabeth thought. She took a deep breath. "My parents told us tonight that you're thinking of coming out here for the holidays," she began, toying nervously with a pencil on her nightstand.

"That's right," Suzanne said. "If you'll even *have* me, that is. I know I was a complete and total monster before, and you have every right to think that I'm the most horrible, the most dreadful, the most—"

Elizabeth took a deep breath. *Don't be fooled*, she warned herself. *You fell for it once and look what happened.*

"You know, Suzanne," she interrupted, "Jessica—remember my twin sister who came out to stay with your parents—Jessica and I were just talking about your arrangements, and we thought you'd be really bored here over Christmas. It really is dull here, you know. No concerts, no nightclubs, no Central Park, no *snow* . . ."

"I think Sweet Valley's a wonderful town," Suzanne said. "You're wrong, Liz. I could never be bored there."

"But this Christmas," Elizabeth continued, "things are going to be particularly bad. I mean it, Suzanne."

"How could things in Sweet Valley ever be bad?" Suzanne asked.

*They'll be more than bad the minute you turn up*, Elizabeth thought. *They'll be rotten!*

"Suzanne," she said calmly, "everyone's already got plans set up for the next two weeks. I know that *I'm* going to be really too busy to spend very much time with you at all. Don't you think that maybe later in the year—say, sometime next summer . . ."

"Liz," Suzanne said, "I want to come out and see you. Are you trying to talk me out of it?"

Elizabeth bit her lip. *Remember what Mom said tonight at dinner*, she told herself unhappily. *Maybe Suzanne really has changed.*

But memories of Suzanne's last visit flooded back, and Elizabeth's resolve strengthened. "I'm just trying to do what would be best for everyone," she said honestly. "And—"

"Well," Suzanne said briskly, "I know I can't convince you on the phone that things are different now. And that's why I've got to come out. Believe me, Liz, you won't be sorry."

"But you'll be so *bored*," Elizabeth repeated. "And so lonesome, so far away from your friends."

"I've never been so excited about a trip before," Suzanne said warmly, ignoring what Elizabeth had said. "And I want you to tell Jessica that, too. I'm going to make everything up to all of you—absolutely everything. Just you wait and see!"

Elizabeth felt sick as she replaced the receiver on the phone. She couldn't believe it.

She wasn't sure why Suzanne was so eager to come out to Sweet Valley for the vacation. But she recognized the tone in her voice and knew the girl must have some ulterior motive. She had sounded so winning, so charming. Just like the girl who had won over the whole town, then caused so much trouble.

They had to come up with some way to stop her from coming—fast!

"OK, so our first plan failed," Jessica said philosophically.

"Jessica, what are you *doing*?" Elizabeth asked, watching in disbelief as her sister squeezed out two wet tea bags into a bowl, lay down on Steven's bed, then placed the tea bags on her closed eyes.

"Puffiness," Jessica told her. "Something in the tea makes your eyelids unpuff. I've got to look my best tomorrow," she reminded Elizabeth. "Suzanne Devlin or no Suzanne Devlin, I want to be on that float next Saturday!"

"It failed miserably." Elizabeth sighed. "She was so excited about the whole thing! Just like the Suzanne we all know and love. All sweetness and light."

"We don't *all* know and love her," Jessica remarked. "Some of us are still waiting for the pleasure of *meeting* this creep."

"Don't move, Jess, you're getting tea on my bedspread," Steven complained.

"We need another plan," Jessica said. "The question is, what can it be?"

Elizabeth giggled. "Jess, who can listen to you when you look so bizarre? If Suzanne could see you now, maybe she'd change her mind."

"I hate to say it," Steven said and sighed, "but I'm afraid we may just have to get used to the idea."

"You're not giving up, are you?" Jessica demanded.

"Well, I'm not sure we've got much choice," Steven admitted. "The thing is, she's supposed to get here the day after tomorrow. What else can we do? Mom and Dad aren't going to help us. And it's obvious that nothing we do or say is going to change Suzanne's mind. We're just going to have to live with it."

"You mean, we're just going to have to save our energy so we can torment her once she's here," Jessica remarked.

"What do you mean?" Elizabeth demanded.

"Look," Jessica said. "Steve's right. We obviously can't stop her from coming. Let her come! Last time you didn't know what she was like. This time you do. And," she added, "this time you have two partners in crime. Right, Steve?"

"We ought to at least—" Elizabeth began.

"No ought-tos," Jessica protested, taking the tea bags off her eyes, sitting up, and blinking a little. "If Suzanne Devlin is so big on coming here, let her come. We'll just make sure she has a

Christmas she'll never forget as long as she lives!"

Elizabeth bit her lip. Then, despite herself, she began to laugh. "You know, Jess," she admitted, "I have a feeling this is going to be one time that I'm really glad I've got a twin sister who knows how to come up with a really evil plan!"

Jessica broke into a smile. "Elizabeth Wakefield," she said as she put the tea bags in the bowl, "you may rest assured. Suzanne Devlin has met her match at last. And you can be sure that when she leaves this house she'll swear she'll never want to come back—not as long as I've still got an ounce of energy left!"

"Then we're decided," Steven said with mock solemnity. "The Terrible Trio has made up its mind at last. We'll let Suzanne Devlin come, and we'll use her visit to punish her for all the rotten things she did before."

"For Mr. Collins," Elizabeth chimed in.

"And for Winston Egbert," Jessica crooned.

"And for *Liz*," Steven pointed out.

Elizabeth suddenly felt uneasy. "I don't know," she said. "Remember what Mom and Dad said about her needing goodwill. Maybe—"

"*Liz*," Jessica said, bouncing up off Steven's bed. "Don't weaken now! *We* know exactly what Suzanne Devlin needs."

"And," she added with a devious smile, "we're going to make sure she gets it. Right?"

"Right!" Steven seconded enthusiastically.

"Right," Elizabeth managed weakly. *Suzanne, she thought, I didn't realize it, but I did you a favor by warning you. If you only knew what's good for you, you'd stay far away!*

# Four

Elizabeth and Steven were sitting together at the kitchen table early Saturday morning, comparing lists of possible Christmas presents. They had just finished breakfast—Steven had made pancakes—and now they were getting down to the serious question of what to give whom.

"What about Todd?" Steven asked curiously. "What are you going to get him? Or have you already got something picked out?"

Elizabeth shook her head, her blond hair tumbling around the shoulders of her terry-cloth bathrobe. Steven had just struck a nerve. For weeks she'd been wondering what sort of gift to get for Todd. The truth of the matter was, she just didn't know.

"I don't want to get him something silly. I care

49

about him too much for that," she confided. "But, I don't know. Now that he's so far away, I'm not sure it would be appropriate to get him something expensive. I was wondering about something like a wallet, but I thought. . . ." Her voice trailed off, and she shrugged.

Steven leaned back in his chair. "Is it my imagination, or do I detect a note of confusion in my younger sister's voice?"

"It's hard," Elizabeth said softly. "Before, Todd and I knew exactly where we stood. He and I were inseparable! And now . . ."

"Are you two as close as you used to be?" Steven asked.

Elizabeth was quiet for a minute. "I think so," she said tentatively. "We're close, I mean, but—"

"But?" Steven repeated, his eyebrows lifting.

Elizabeth shook her head. "Sometimes I'm not sure what kind of closeness it is anymore," she admitted. "I love getting letters from him, and when he calls it's still the high point of the day. You know, Todd's been my best friend—my best *male* friend—for ages. But sometimes lately I wonder . . ."

"You think the romance is turning into friendship?" Steven asked gently.

Elizabeth thought for a few minutes. "I really don't know," she said at last. "I guess we've been so far away from each other that neither of us really knows *what* we feel. All I can tell you is

50

that I can't wait to see him again to find out. I've missed him *so* much . . ."

"I'm hopeful for you two," Steven said softly, affectionately rumpling Elizabeth's hair. "I know the distance makes everything hard, but if any couple can pull through it, I think you and Todd can."

"Still," Elizabeth mused, "I don't know what to do about a Christmas present. Somehow I just don't really feel right, giving him a wallet. I need to think of something a little less extravagant. And I just don't know . . ."

"Don't know what?" Jessica demanded from the doorway.

"What," Steven gasped, doubling up with laughter, "in God's name are you doing in that *costume*, Jess? Have you completely and totally lost your marbles, or is this supposed to be some kind of joke?"

Elizabeth spun around to see what her brother was laughing at. "I don't believe it!" she gasped, her hand flying to her mouth as her blue-green eyes widened with astonishment.

Jessica was dressed as an elf. She was wearing kelly green tights and green slippers with curled-up toes and bells jangling from their tips. She had made a strange little suit out of a green plastic garbage bag, cutting leg holes in the bottom and arm holes in the sides and stapling the whole thing up at the shoulders. Something—probably newspaper, from the look of it—was

51

being used as stuffing to make her look round. Underneath the sack she wore a red long-sleeved T-shirt. There was green paint on her face. "I need some sort of hat," Jessica announced calmly, ignoring the looks on her brother's and sister's faces. "What's the matter?" she added, taking a small green plastic tomato basket out of the trash and tying long red ribbons on each side. "Hasn't either of you ever seen an elf before?"

"Jessica," Elizabeth gasped, "why in the world are you dressed that way? Have you gone nuts?"

"It just so happens," Jessica said haughtily, placing the plastic basket on her head like a hat and tying the ribbons underneath her chin, "that *I* have volunteered to be an elf at the mall today. I'm going to help Santa pass presents out to all the little kids."

"Why?" Steven asked, wiping tears of laughter from his cheeks. "I thought you were going to be Miss Christmastime today and wear tea bags on your eyes!"

"You don't know anything," Jessica retorted. "The Miss Christmastime selection isn't until this afternoon. I'll have plenty of time to get out of this costume by then."

"But, Jess," Elizabeth asked, *"why*? This doesn't seem like your idea of a good way to spend a Saturday morning. Not the first Saturday of vacation, anyway. I would have thought . . ."

"Cara talked me into it," Jessica admitted, traipsing across the room with her curly toes extended. "I have to admit I've got misgivings about the whole thing," she added, arranging her stuffing so she could sit down. "But Cara was insistent. She was supposed to do it, but she called me late last night and said she couldn't go through with it because she'd come down with a rotten cold. It's a sorority thing," she added, stretching her legs out so the bells rang on her toes.

"I should have guessed," Elizabeth said. At her sister's insistence, Elizabeth had joined Pi Beta Alpha, the most exclusive sorority at school. But she had never been very involved. She thought most of the girls were snobs, and she was a member in name only.

Jessica, on the other hand, was a dedicated member. "It never hurts," she once explained to Elizabeth, "to stay involved with the prettiest, most fun-loving bunch of girls in the whole school. Don't you realize how much I owe to that sorority?"

"Probably about seventeen dollars," Elizabeth had said, thinking of the expensive dues the active members were asked to pay at the beginning of each term of school.

"You see, every year Pi Beta Alpha sends someone over to the mall to help Santa pass out gifts," Jessica was explaining now, ignoring the mirth on her brother's face. "Cara was supposed to be the elf this year. It's really a very responsible position," she added defensively.

"I'm sure it is." Elizabeth smiled. "How many hours do you have to work?"

"I'm not sure," Jessica struggled to get to her feet without crushing the stuffing in her costume. "I just hope it doesn't run into the Miss Christmastime contest. Cara promised it wouldn't, and I'd hate to have to leave early, but at two-thirty I've got to run over to the civic center, no matter what."

"Maybe you'd better take your makeup off before you go," Steven suggested, winking at Elizabeth. "Sweet Valley's never had a Miss Christmastime with green skin before!"

"Very funny," Jessica snorted, tromping out of the kitchen. A few minutes later she returned. "Hey!" she exclaimed. "Look at this! It was out on the front porch!"

"Your first Secret Santa present!" Elizabeth exclaimed. It was a small package, wrapped in red-and-green plaid paper, with JESSICA spelled out across it in green ribbon.

"Open it up," Steven said eagerly. "Come on, Jess. I don't have a Secret Santa, so I have to get a vicarious thrill from yours."

But no one had to urge Jessica to open her gift. Within seconds she had torn off the wrapping paper, and she was staring with openmouthed

54

amazement at a little wooden jewel box, not much bigger than her hand. "Wow!" she exclaimed, setting it down on the kitchen counter and opening the lid. A familiar tune began as soon as the lid had been lifted. "That's *Für Elise*, by Beethoven," Elizabeth exclaimed, jumping up to have a look. "Oh, Jess, what a wonderful present!"

"It's from Hans, isn't it?" Jessica said happily, hugging the jewel box to her. "Nobody else could ever have picked such a classy present. It's definitely Hans. You can just see the European taste written all over this!"

*Oh, dear,* Elizabeth thought. *I don't know who Jess's Secret Santa is, but I know for sure it isn't Hans.*

"Besides," Jessica continued, "Beethoven was German, wasn't he? It's a dead giveaway!"

Watching her twin try to dance across the kitchen floor, jewel box in hand, Elizabeth began to laugh. "Jess, if the Pageant Committee could see you now, I think they'd have you locked up!"

"See you two later," Jessica said airily. "And the next time I see you, I'll be able to tell you the good news: that I'll be Miss Christmastime for sure!"


Jessica had never guessed being an elf could be so tiring. It was only two o'clock, and already her face ached from smiling. She was beginning to get a headache from the excited cries of the children lined up in front of Santa's house in the middle of the mall.

Santa, a kindly faced, snowy-haired man in his late sixties, was wonderful with the children. "Ho-ho-ho!" he boomed, ringing a little bell each time a child came up to sit on his lap. Jessica was the one who handed each child a present, when she wasn't back in the dark interior of the house itself, scrambling around for the next gift.

"When's the replacement elf coming?" Jessica asked Santa hopefully at about two-fifteen. She hated to be rude, but it was time for her to get moving if she was going to get all the green paint off her face before the contest started.

"What replacement?" Santa asked, looking baffled.

"You know," Jessica said anxiously, yanking the newspapers up so her belly wouldn't sag. "The second shift."

Santa laughed. "There isn't one," he said merrily. "You're all I've got, Jessica. Don't tell me you're getting tired already!"

Jessica's heart skipped a beat. "You mean . . . how long do you want me to stay here?" she asked, fighting to keep her voice calm.

Santa took out his pocket watch and scratched his head. "Santa's house doesn't shut until five," he told her. "I'd sure hate to have to close down early and disappoint so many children."

Jessica followed his gaze to the long line of

children still waiting to sit on Santa's lap. An overwhelming feeling of disappointment swept over her. She couldn't possibly leave! Santa needed her, and if she backed out now, he'd have to close down his house and break all these poor kids' hearts.

Jessica was fighting hard not to burst into tears. "Can I just run and make one phone call?" she begged Santa. "I promise I'll just be a minute. Don't worry, I'm not going to desert you," she promised, seeing the crestfallen expression on the kindly old man's face. "I'll be back in two seconds. I promise."

"OK, Cara," she seethed several minutes later from a public telephone. "What's the idea? You told me to be at the mall at twelve—and only for an hour or two! But Santa needs me all day. And I have to be at the civic center at three o'clock!"

Cara was astonished. "What do you mean? You won't be able to try out for Miss Christmas-time?" she said when Jessica had managed to get the whole story out. "Jess, that's terrible! I didn't know that! I never would have agreed to make you—"

"Agreed to make me *what*?" Jessica shrieked. "Cara Walker, if you want to ever recover from what I suspect is a fake cold anyway, you'd better tell me what's going on here."

Cara sounded tearful. "It wasn't my fault," she said miserably. "You'd better call Lila. She's the one who put me up to it. But *she* had all the information, Jess. I didn't know being an elf for the day would keep you from being Miss Christmastime—honest! Lila said it would just be a silly joke, that you'd just have to wear green paint for a couple of hours. Honest, Jess . . ."

"OK, Cara," Jessica said wearily. "I've got to go help Santa out, but I want to try to get hold of Lila first. *I'm going to kill her.*"

But no one was home at Lila's when Jessica called. That was what Eva, the Fowlers' housekeeper, explained when she picked up the phone. "Do you have any idea," Jessica said furiously, "where Lila happens to be and what time she's due home?"

"Miss Fowler's already left for the Christmas pageant," Eva told her. "She said she'd be there for at least two hours. Can I leave her a message?"

Jessica, her hand quivering with rage, slammed the receiver on its hook without a word.

*I've been had,* she thought, storming back down the mall toward Santa's house.

Her dream of being Miss Christmastime was completely ruined. If she deserted Santa she'd give the sorority a bad name forever. She was stuck; she didn't have a choice.

"Jessica, you're back!" Santa said eagerly. "Thank heavens! Now if you'll just stand here and pass a gift to each little boy and girl as they come up to sit on my lap . . ."

58

Jessica gave Santa a sickly smile.

*Something tells me*, she thought miserably, looking with dismay at the long line of mothers and little children that had formed while she was away, *that this is going to be a day to remember. And Lila Fowler can be certain that when she's done with her little triumph this afternoon, she's going to pay for setting me up this way!*

"Jessica Wakefield," Santa said triumphantly when the last child had left with his mother, "you've been a wonderful elf. I can't tell you how delightful it's been to work with you."

"Thanks," Jessica said, dispirited. She was glad she'd made Santa happy, but she couldn't feel good just then. All she could think about was the contest at the civic center.

"Is something wrong?" Santa asked suddenly, noticing the crestfallen look on her face.

The next minute Jessica found herself telling Santa the whole story. "Oh, dear. Oh, *dear*," he kept saying. "Well, good heavens. Why didn't you tell me you needed to leave so badly?"

"I didn't want to let you down," Jessica said glumly. "And now everything's ruined, and I'll never get to ride on a float in the parade!"

Santa's blue eyes twinkled as he looked Jessica up and down. "I've got an idea," he said slowly, "though it isn't as glamorous as being Miss Christmastime. How would you like to ride on

59

*my* float next Saturday? I could always use another elf in a big parade like that!"

Jessica stared at him. "You mean—ride on a float dressed like this?" She stared down at her curled toes and bulging stomach with disbelief.

"Why not?" Santa asked.

Jessica thought quickly. She couldn't imagine anything worse than humiliating herself in public in this costume. After she'd dreamed for so long of wearing a gown, with her hair flowing around her shoulders . . .

Suddenly Jessica's face lit up. She had just had a wonderful idea.

A wonderful, terrible idea.

"Santa," she exclaimed, "that's a wonderful suggestion! Count me in." She chuckled. She had just thought of a wonderful way to get even with Lila Fowler.

And she owed everything to good old Santa.


"What happened to you?" Elizabeth demanded, squelching the urge to laugh when she saw how miserable her sister looked as she dragged herself upstairs.

"I don't want to talk about it," Jessica muttered. "Let me just tell you, this was the worst day ever. The very worst day of my entire life. I'm going up to take a hot bath and get out of this ridiculous costume!"

Elizabeth followed Jessica up the steps. "Poor

Jess," she commiserated. "Did they make you work really hard?"

"I was framed," Jessica said, yanking off her green slippers and hurling them into her bedroom. Elizabeth could hear the little bells jangle as they hit the floor.

"What do you mean, *framed*?" Elizabeth demanded. "Did you make it over to the pageant, or—"

Something stopped Elizabeth from finishing her question. "I guess not," she told herself, seeing the look on Jessica's face.

"That Lila Fowler," Jessica raged as she went into the bathroom and turned on the water in the tub full force. Then she walked over to the sink and began slathering her face with cold cream. She scrubbed the green paint off with angry motions. "She *won* the stupid pageant, and I hope she's happy."

"What are you talking about?" Elizabeth asked. "How could she—"

"She had all the information on being an elf," Jessica told her. "And she lied to Cara and convinced her to play a trick on me. Now I'm supposed to be an elf on his float in the parade!"

Elizabeth fought back the urge to laugh. "And Lila won because you were eliminated," she finished, sitting on the edge of the bathtub. "You must be really furious!"

"I am," Jessica replied, ripping open the green trash bag and yanking newspapers out. "But I've already figured out exactly how I'm going to get even."

"Which is?"

"Next week," Jessica explained, "before the parade, I'm going to steal Lila's crown. *And* her dress. And I'm going to dress up as Miss Christmastime and leave my elf costume right where Lila's dress was, in the changing room at the civic center. There'll be nothing she can do about it, because if she makes a scene, everyone will find out what she did. And she'll be too afraid of getting the sorority in trouble if she disappoints Santa. So Lila"—Jessica burst out laughing—"will have the pleasure of wearing green paint in public. And not me!"

Elizabeth sighed. "You two deserve each other. Though I have to admit it's a pretty good idea," she added. "What a rat. I can't believe she did that to you!"

"Meanwhile, I'm just *pretending* to be upset so she won't suspect I'm going to get back at her." Jessica giggled.

"Girls!" Mrs. Wakefield called, knocking on the door. "Can I come in?"

"Sure, Mom," Jessica said.

"What in God's name *is* all this stuff?" Mrs. Wakefield asked, her brow wrinkling with confusion as she looked at the newspaper and the shredded garbage bag strewn on the bathroom floor.

"I'll clean it up, Mom," Jessica said contritely. "It was left over from my elf suit."

"From your . . ." Mrs. Wakefield shook her head in disbelief. "Never mind," she said. "Honestly, Jess. This time I think I'd just rather not know."

"But, Mom—"

"Listen, you two. I'm trying to get things organized for Suzanne," Mrs. Wakefield said quickly. "I know it's a bit of a sore point, but we need to figure out where she's going to sleep. Jess, I thought maybe you and Liz could double up in Liz's room and Suzanne could stay in your room."

"Why not?" Jessica said, aggrieved. "Everything else in the whole world is going so well, why *shouldn't* I get kicked out of my room for the whole vacation?"

"Please." Mrs. Wakefield sighed. "You're not making this any easier. It's the best place, Jess."

"She stayed in my room *last* time," Jessica reminded her mother, "and the place smelled like perfume for months."

"Jess," Mrs. Wakefield said firmly, "you've got to try cleaning it up tonight. Honestly. The way it looks right now, I couldn't ask *anyone* to stay in there. Clothes all over the floor, your entire dresser emptied onto the bed . . ."

Jessica looked injured. She was used to hearing her room criticized, but she thought it was wonderful—full of personality. On a whim she had painted the walls chocolate brown one rainy Saturday, and Elizabeth always claimed that it looked like a cross between a mud pit and a rummage sale. But Jessica didn't care. She liked it just the way it was.

"I mean it, Jess," Mrs. Wakefield repeated, shaking her head again as she looked at the bathroom. "I'm counting on its looking presentable by tomorrow morning."

"Liz!" Jessica gasped as soon as their mother had closed the door behind her. "Don't you see how absolutely *perfect* this is?"

"What?" Elizabeth asked. "Having to share my bedroom for the next two weeks with the Jolly Green Giant?"

Jessica looked cross. "OK, *be* that way," she muttered, turning the water off in the tub.

"OK, OK," Elizabeth conceded. "Tell me what you mean, Jess. I'm all ears."

"Mom just gave me a brilliant idea," Jessica burst out, her eyes shining. "She asked me to get the room ready for Devil-face Devlin. Right?"

"Right." Elizabeth laughed. "So what?"

"So." Jessica said, "we'll get it ready. We'll make sure Suzanne has a room waiting for her that she'll never believe!"

Suddenly Elizabeth caught on. "We'll be little elves," she teased her twin.

"Secret Santas," Jessica corrected her. "Only instead of presents, we're going to give her a lump of coal in her stocking."

"Burned-out bulbs in the lamps," Elizabeth suggested.

"We'll short-sheet her bed," Jessica hissed "and plant horrible things in all the corners of the room and—"

"Jessica," Elizabeth confessed, shaking her head, "I'm glad I'm not Suzanne Devlin. That's all I can say. I have a feeling this poor girl is going to go absolutely crazy by the time she's been here three days!"

"And I," Jessica said happily, "have a feeling that you've never spoken truer words, Elizabeth Wakefield, in your entire life. Suzanne Devlin is in for the worst Christmas holiday she's ever had!"

# Five

"Come on, Liz," Jessica said, her face wrinkling with irritation. "Hans is going to be here tonight, and I told him I'd meet him *ages* ago!"

The twins were in the parking lot of the Dairi Burger, a hamburger spot that was a favorite meeting place for Sweet Valley High students. It had all the right ingredients to make it fun on a weekend night: a good jukebox, wonderful burgers and shakes, and large booths.

That night a kind of informal gathering from school was taking place inside the crowded restaurant. Elizabeth recognized dozens of familiar faces as she went through the door with her sister. "Liz, Jess—over here!" Ken Matthews called, waving from three small tables that had been pushed together in the back. Elizabeth followed Jessica, though following Jessica meant stopping every two feet to say hello to someone. As usual Jessica was managing to get mileage out of her escapade at the mall that day. She told everybody about it, embroidering the details so that it sounded even sillier than it actually had been.

"Whew!" Elizabeth laughed when they had finally made it to the back of the restaurant. People moved their chairs so that Jessica and Elizabeth could squeeze in. Ten was a few too many for a comfortable fit, but comfort wasn't the most important thing. A holiday atmosphere was prevailing, and what mattered was being together.

Ken was sitting with Aaron Dallas and Aaron's new girlfriend, Patsy Webber, who was squished between them, dwarfed by their big shoulders. Olivia Davidson and her boyfriend Roger Patman were sitting next to each other. The twins had squeezed in next to Winston Egbert and Enid Rollins, who was there with a date, an outgoing, brown-eyed freshman from Sweet Valley College named Chip Ettelson.

Jessica was scanning the restaurant eagerly for Hans, who was either late or hidden in a far booth. "Hey, Jess, has your Secret Santa been good to you?" Winston asked suddenly, winking at Ken.

"He sure has," Jessica said smugly. "He's obviously a man of incredible taste." *Not like some*

68

*people,* her look clearly said. Winston flushed. He had once had a crush on Jessica and still seemed to be strongly affected by her.

"I got a five-pound bag of red pistachio nuts today," Patsy said, giggling. "Aaron is going to get jealous if my Secret Santa's this attentive all week."

"I got a coupon for a free back rub from mine." Aaron grinned. "I can't wait to find out who it is."

"Speaking of surprises," Jessica said, catching her twin's eye, "I'm afraid Liz and I have a real bombshell to drop. You tell them, Liz."

"No." Elizabeth sighed. "I can't stand to be the bearer of bad news. You tell them, Jess."

"*Somebody* tell us!" Patsy Webber wailed. "I'm dying of suspense!"

"OK, OK," Jessica said, looking serious. "But remember, we warned you. It isn't good."

"Jessica . . ." Ken said threateningly.

"All right!" Jessica yelped. "Guess who's coming to town?" she asked.

"Beats me," Winston said.

"Santa Claus!" Patsy Webber piped up.

"Suzanne Devlin," Jessica told them. "Tomorrow. And she's staying for two whole weeks!"

"Arrrrggghhh!" Winston exclaimed, burying his head in his hands. "We're ruined!"

"The plague," Ken Matthews said. "We're being visited by the plague."

Aaron groaned. "I can't stand it. I knew everything was too good around here. How can you guys possibly let that monster come back?"

"We can't help it," Elizabeth said. "She's told my parents she wants to visit. Supposedly she wants to apologize in person, to make up with everyone."

"Fat chance," Winston muttered. "She's probably just sick of making everyone on the East Coast miserable and thought she'd spread the wealth."

"I feel horrible about it," Elizabeth told them. "It's bad enough that *we* have to suffer. But to inflict her on you guys again . . ."

"Who," Chip asked innocently, "is Suzanne Devlin?"

The whole group was quiet for a second, and then everyone burst out laughing. "I'll explain the whole thing to you later," Enid told him. "Otherwise, it'll spoil our appetites."

"Suzanne Devlin," Winston informed him, "is without a doubt the craftiest, most manipulative, most—"

"Gorgeous," Olivia supplied for him.

"Most gorgeous," Winston repeated, shaking his head, "most *impossible* girl on the whole earth. She's bad news with a capital *B*. She's a pain in the neck with a capital *P*. She's—"

Chip laughed. "I get the idea. Why's she coming back if she's so popular around here?"

"That's a good question," Elizabeth said. "To be honest, we're not sure. But we figure—"

"We'd rather spend our time making sure she won't come back," Jessica finished.

"Two weeks." Winston groaned. "I don't think the town will last that long under siege. Isn't there some way to stop her?"

Elizabeth sighed. "No. I'm afraid we're just going to have to put up with her."

"Well," Aaron said, putting his arm around Patsy and giving her a hug, "let us know if you need help giving her a rough time. We're ready. Aren't we, Winston?"

Elizabeth looked horrified. It was one thing for her and Jessica to plan pranks. But to involve anybody else . . .

"We owe it to her to at least be civil," she told Aaron. "I mean, we can't—"

"Thanks, Aaron," Jessica interrupted. "We always knew we could count on you if things got really awful!"

"Jessica!" Elizabeth gasped, but it was too late. Jessica had just caught sight of Hans, who was coming in the door with Bruce Patman, and she was off like a flash, her most flirtatious smile on her face.

*My sister*, Elizabeth thought, *is absolutely impossible.*

"Don't worry, Liz," Enid said warmly, sensing, as she always could, when her friend was upset. "I'm sure things with Suzanne won't be as bad as they were last time."

"How could they be?" Winston pointed out. "*Nothing* could possibly be as bad as last time."

"I hope not," Elizabeth said, watching Jessica out of the corner of her eye.

She wished Winston were right. But with Jessica on the rampage, Elizabeth couldn't be sure.

And there was nothing that Elizabeth or anyone else could do.


Elizabeth was engrossed in a conversation with Patsy when she realized that the whole restaurant had suddenly fallen quiet. She wondered what had caused everyone to stop talking.

Turning around, she followed the eyes of her schoolmates, who were looking at the Dairi Burger entrance.

It was the Sweet Valley High swim team, led by Bill Chase, an attractive, blond junior, whose surfing expertise had won him a fan club at school. But that wasn't what was making everyone stare in silence.

The guys were wearing only bathing suits! Each had a towel around his neck, and they were walking together in a line, each with his hand on the shoulder of the guy in front of him. It was the most hilarious performance Elizabeth had ever seen.

And they were heading right for her table!

"Olivia Davidson," Stan Richards called out,

stepping forward with a mock bow, "your Secret Santa has instructed us to serenade you."

Olivia turned beet red. "Omigod," she gasped, clapping her hands to her face. "Oh, no! Tell me this isn't happening!"

But it *was* happening. Stan blew a note on a pitch pipe, Bill Chase chimed in with him, and the next moment all ten guys were singing "Silent Night" while the crowd that had gathered screamed encouragement. Elizabeth had never seen anyone turn as red as Olivia.

"Stop them," she begged, hiding her face against Roger's shoulder. "Roger, make them *stop!*"

But it was obvious the swimmers' choir was having far too good a time to stop. For the next ten minutes they entertained the restaurant with no fewer than five Christmas carols—some more off-key than others, but all more or less recognizable.

After her initial embarrassment, even Olivia enjoyed the show. By the time the swimmers were done serenading her, she was begging them to stay as loudly as all her classmates.

"Amazing," Enid said, shaking her head as the swim team walked away. "Whoever would have thought the swim team had that much musical talent?"

Elizabeth just shook her head. She was wondering what Mr. Collins would say if he realized how exotic the Secret Santa gifts were becoming.

"Hey, Liz," Ken joked, waving his straw at her like a baton, "I'll bet you can't wait till Todd gets back!"

Elizabeth blushed as everyone turned to stare at her.

"That's right," Winston said, whistling. "The star-crossed lovers will be reunited any day now. Let's see if our on-the-spot interview for Channel Five can reveal the hidden emotions Ms. Wakefield is experiencing right now!" Adopting a television reporter's voice, Winston grabbed the straw out of Ken's hand to represent a microphone. "Tell us, Ms. Wakefield, will you be glad to see Mr. Wilkins when he gets into town on Monday?"

"Cut it out, Winston." Elizabeth laughed and pushed the straw away as he thrust it toward her. She didn't feel like joking about Todd's imminent visit. In fact, she didn't feel like talking about it at all.

"What's the matter?" Enid asked her later when the two girls were alone out in the parking lot. Enid was waiting for Chip to make a phone call, and Elizabeth was waiting for Jessica to finish flirting—for the night anyway—with Hans.

"Nothing." Elizabeth smiled. "I just feel kind of—I don't know—kind of quiet right now. You know what I mean?"

"I do," she said quietly. "It's Todd, isn't it?" she asked.

Elizabeth nodded. "I guess I'm a little ner-

74

vous," she admitted. "I've been looking forward to seeing him again for so long, but now that it's really almost here . . ."

"Everything's going to be fine," Enid told her. "Don't worry about a thing, kiddo. You know you two will see fireworks the minute you hold each other in your arms!"

Elizabeth sighed. "Maybe you're right," she said. "The truth is, I'm just afraid that I might be expecting too much, you know?"

Enid shook her head. "You and Todd are like bread and butter," she told her confidently. "You belong together! Now, quit worrying! The minute Todd gets here everything will be all right. I just know it."

"How's Chip?" Elizabeth asked curiously, dropping her voice a little. "He's really adorable!"

"Isn't he?" Enid smiled. "He's sweet. Maybe a little too sweet. But so far, so good. This is only our second date, and I never feel like I can tell what's going on till I've spent some time with a guy."

"I know what you mean," Elizabeth agreed.

"Oh, look. Chip's done with his phone call," Enid said, catching sight of her date coming out of the Dairi Burger. "I'd better run. Where's Jess?"

"God knows," Elizabeth said, getting annoyed. "If she doesn't come out soon, I'll have to go in and get her."

75

Chip and Enid kept her company, and a minute later, Jessica strolled out, a radiant smile on her face.

"Sorry," she said lightly, grabbing the keys out of Elizabeth's hand and slipping into the driver's seat of the Fiat. Elizabeth made a face at Enid and Chip. "Sisters!" she said, hurrying around to the passenger side. "Thanks for waiting with me, you two!"

"Liz, I'm in love!" Jessica declared when Elizabeth got into the car.

"Hans?" Elizabeth asked.

"He's so wonderful, Liz." Jessica sighed. "Those foreigners really know how to kiss." She started the car up. "What do you think, Liz? Can you see me living in a castle somewhere in Bavaria?"

"Sounds like a horror movie." Elizabeth laughed. "You and Baron von Frankenstein deep in the Bavarian woods. When are you two planning to move to Germany together?"

"I don't know," Jessica admitted. She looked nonplussed. "I forgot to ask him." A shudder ran through her as she backed the Fiat out of the parking lot. "I certainly wouldn't want to let him go back without me if we really *do* fall in love. No offense, Liz, but I don't see how you and Todd can stand this long-distance stuff."

"What do you mean?"

Jessica shrugged. "I don't know. It's just always seemed to me that being tied down is

76

only worth it if you really get to see each other. With him in Vermont and you here . . ."

"But Todd and I aren't really tied down," Elizabeth protested. "We're both free to date. You know that, Jess."

Jessica wrinkled her nose. "Date? When was the last time you really went out on a *date*? Sure, you get someone to go with you if there's a big dance or something. But Todd's the only guy you care about. Admit it."

Elizabeth sighed. "Can I help it if I'm slow, Jess? I just can't imagine caring for more than one guy at a time."

Jessica digested that thought for a minute as she drove. "True," she said after a while. "I suppose *I* never care for more than one guy at a time, either. It's just that mine seem to have a quicker turnover rate." She giggled. "You and Todd . . . you two seem practically married. Only he's in Vermont, and you're here. What a mess!"

Elizabeth laughed. She was used to hearing her love life analyzed by her twin. Still, it *had* been a long time since she had been on her own—really on her own, without Todd to think about. She wondered now how it would feel to get excited about seeing some guy in the hall, to spend hours getting ready to go out . . .

"Of course," Jessica was saying, "the thing about long-distance love is that it's very romantic. You must be so excited about seeing Todd on

Monday. Are you going to meet him at the airport?"

"No," Elizabeth said. "Ken and his father are going to pick him up, and I thought I'd stay home so I could see him alone."

"What time will he be here?"

Elizabeth shook her head. "He's calling tomorrow night to let me know the exact time."

"I wonder," Jessica said thoughtfully, "what people think about Todd at his new school. Do you suppose he's really popular?"

Elizabeth laughed. "Do you mean with girls? I'm sure he is," she said lightly. She couldn't imagine him without a group of close friends—both girls and boys. She knew he thrived on company and would be miserable without an active social life. But what about girls as more than friends?

"Tell me the truth, Liz," Jessica said as she turned into the Wakefields' driveway. She sounded unusually serious. "I've always been afraid to ask, but I really want to know how you feel. What would you do if Todd fell in love with someone in Vermont?"

Elizabeth didn't know what to say. It was a question she had asked herself before but never answered. And she was speechless now.

"I thought so," Jessica said, staring at her. "You'd be miserable," she concluded, turning off the engine. "I just had to ask."

*Why couldn't I answer?* Elizabeth wondered,

following Jessica into the house. *Would I really feel so strongly if Todd told me he'd fallen in love with some other girl?*

Elizabeth didn't know. All she hoped was that she and Todd could relax together, that they could try to pick things up from where they'd left off. Anything further than that, Elizabeth reasoned, was simply too much to ask at this point.

# Six

"Announcing the arrival of flight six-seventeen from New York's Kennedy Airport," a voice over the loudspeaker said smoothly.

Alice Wakefield sighed as she waited for Suzanne. She couldn't help wishing one of the twins had come along, though she hadn't asked either of them and she wasn't surprised that they hadn't volunteered. This was a task she would gladly have shared with somebody. *What on earth am I going to say to the girl?* she wondered. She couldn't help remembering how tense things had been the previous spring, when she and Ned had driven Suzanne back to the airport after her disastrous visit. Mrs. Wakefield had found it hard to believe a girl of sixteen could have behaved that way. She, too, had been fooled by

Suzanne. And she had been sorely disappointed in what had proven to be the girl's true character. *Still, under the circumstances . . .* she reminded herself, shaking her head as she remembered the story Tom Devlin had unfolded the other night on the phone.

*Poor Suzanne,* she thought now. *I hope she's prepared for what I'm sure is lying in store for her these next two weeks. I wonder if she has any idea . . .*

Mrs. Wakefield's reverie was interrupted by the surge of passengers walking toward her. "Mrs. Wakefield!" Suzanne called, waving from behind a group of people.

Mrs. Wakefield knew that Suzanne would look different. "She's lost some weight," Tom Devlin had said, "and her color's bad from the medication." Sure enough, Suzanne looked much thinner. She was still outstandingly beautiful, her long black hair slightly less lustrous, perhaps, but attractively arranged in a long french braid. Her skin was so pale it looked translucent, and Mrs. Wakefield could detect the faint outline of veins in her forehead.

She looked fragile, Mrs. Wakefield thought. Fragile, but lovely.

"Thank you for coming all the way out here to get me," Suzanne said, putting down the oversize bag she was carrying to embrace Mrs. Wakefield.

"Let's go down and get your luggage." Mrs. Wakefield smiled, trying to sound natural.

Suzanne laughed. "This is all I brought," she admitted, waving at her bag. "I thought I'd travel light this time."

"OK, then," Mrs. Wakefield said. "Let's go get the car!"

Surprisingly, the ride from the airport was extremely enjoyable. Mrs. Wakefield couldn't get over the change in Suzanne. She was much quieter than she had been before, and a good deal of her vivacious energy seemed to have been drained from her. But she was wonderful to talk to—pleasant, polite, and astonishingly relaxed. It was as if she'd come to terms with something since the last time she'd been out there, and wasn't trying anymore to put on a performance. She was simply being herself, and she seemed at peace.

"I'd better warn you," Mrs. Wakefield said quietly as she turned off the expressway. "This isn't going to be easy, Suzanne. I admire you for having the courage to come out here, and I think I understand why you want to go through with it. Mr. Collins told us about the letter you sent him, and I know he's forgiven you. But I have a feeling things are going to be rough for you. Are you sure you're up to it?"

Suzanne stared out the window, and when she looked back at Mrs. Wakefield, her eyes were filled with tears. "I hope so," she said quietly. "I have no way of knowing before I try."

"Well," Mrs. Wakefield said, sighing, "Ned and I will do what we can, but I'm afraid—"

"No, Mrs. Wakefield," Suzanne interrupted. "I've got to do this on my own. You two have done more than enough just by letting me come out here. The rest is up to me."

*Well*, Mrs. Wakefield thought, *I wish I felt better about what's about to happen. But I know Liz was terribly hurt by Suzanne before, and so were most of the kids she knows. And I have a feeling that they're not going to be easy on Suzanne.*

*If only she hadn't sworn us to secrecy*, Alice Wakefield thought. *If the kids knew—if they had any idea . . .*

But Suzanne had made herself perfectly clear. No one was to be told a single thing. She wanted to fight this battle herself. She didn't want pity. She wanted to win everyone over on her own terms, to make up with them all without anyone's help.

She wished Suzanne luck, Alice Wakefield thought sadly. But it wasn't going to be easy. In fact, knowing what she knew about her own children, she had a feeling this was going to be one battle Suzanne wouldn't be able to win.


"They're here!" Jessica hissed, racing from her spot at the window. "They're *here*!"

Mr. Wakefield was out running errands, and Elizabeth, Jessica, and Steven were alone in the house, waiting for Suzanne and Mrs. Wakefield to get back from the airport. "Now, remember," Jessica warned, "*no* pity. If she acts nice, she's just trying to trick all of us. So don't back down and be nice, no matter what!"

"We're home!" Mrs. Wakefield called a minute later from the living room.

Jessica put her finger to her lips. "Remember," she hissed. "Act like we forgot she was coming, OK?"

"Jessica? Elizabeth?" Mrs. Wakefield called, sounding confused. "I don't know where they are," she said to Suzanne, her voice slightly irritated. "I told them we'd be here about now, and they said—Jessica! Steven! Where are you guys?"

"I'll go down first," Jessica whispered.

"What is it, Mom?" she called down the steps, her voice casual.

"What do you mean, what is it?" Mrs. Wakefield called back. "Suzanne's here, and I'd like you to all come downstairs and say hello to her. That's what it is!"

"Suzanne?" Jessica said vaguely, taking her time coming downstairs. "Oh, Suz*anne*," she said, coming into the living room. "God, I completely forgot! I'm so embarrassed!"

"Suzanne, this is Jessica," Mrs. Wakefield said, giving her daughter a murderous look. "I'm sorry. I don't know where Steve is, or Liz. *Jessica—*"

85

"You must be exhausted," Jessica said sweetly, extending her hand as if to shake hands with Suzanne. "How long does it take to fly here from Miami?"

"Miami?" Suzanne said, staring at Jessica. "You mean New York."

"Jessica—" Mrs. Wakefield said warningly.

Jessica clapped her hand to her forehead. "What was I *thinking* of," she asked an invisible audience. "Of *course*. You're from New York! I stayed in your parents' apartment!"

"That's right," Suzanne said, looking at her a little strangely. "And you met some of my friends, I think, if I—"

"Your friends," Jessica said, flinging herself down on the sofa and reaching for a piece of candy from the bowl on the coffee table, "were the most *fascinating*, the most *wonderful*—"

"Suzanne," Elizabeth said breathlessly, running into the room. "I'm so sorry. I was on the phone, and I couldn't—"

"Liz!" Suzanne exclaimed, hurrying over and embracing Elizabeth. "I'm so glad to see you again!"

Mrs. Wakefield shook her head. "Suzanne, I'm going to take your bag upstairs," she said flatly. "We're going to put you in Jessica's room again, if that's OK."

"It's fine with me," Suzanne said, "if it's OK with Jessica. I mean it's—"

"I am *honored*," Jessica insisted as her mother left the room, "Absolutely honored."

"You're all so nice," Suzanne began again, somewhat lamely, "to let me come out here and impose myself on you when it's your vacation and everything. I know I'm—"

"Nonsense," Jessica exclaimed with false heartiness. "We've been looking forward to it for days, Suzy. Isn't that what people call you— Suzy?"

Suzanne took a deep breath. "Yes, they do—" she began.

"Oh, hello, Suzanne," Steven remarked casually, coming into the room and standing at one end of the couch, looking at Suzanne without smiling.

"Well," Suzanne said at last, when it became apparent that was all he was going to say, "it's nice to see you again."

Steven stared at her, raising his eyebrows slightly, and remained silent.

*This is unbearable*, Elizabeth thought. *How can the poor girl stand it?*

"How was your flight?" she said finally, unable to bear the tense silence a moment longer.

"OK," Suzanne said, looking relieved and smiling at Elizabeth. "You know—sort of boring."

"Of course," Jessica said significantly, "it's different for us out here, Suzy. We're used to

87

being bored. Aren't we, Liz? In fact just the other day I was saying to Steve, you know, we'll have to take a nice airplane ride somewhere soon to interrupt this boring spell we're having."

"That's right," Steven cut in. "It must be different for you, Suzanne, living right in the middle of New York City."

Suzanne blushed. "Well, it's kind of—"

"Divine," Jessica interrupted. "What a frantic pace you all keep up in the big city! Good heavens," she exclaimed, "I was positively worn *out* by the exertion! Your friend Pete—"

"He isn't my 'friend' anymore," Suzanne said flatly. "Jessica, I'm sorry about what happened. You must have been really upset."

"Upset?" Jessica's eyebrows shot up. "Well, it's true I'm not used to that sort of thing," she said sweetly. "Out here in small-town America, that sort of thing just doesn't *happen* every day. But all the same—"

"Maybe I'd better go upstairs and wash up," Suzanne said suddenly. "Will you excuse me? I'll be down in a few minutes."

"We'll be right here," Jessica sang out, flashing Suzanne her most sickeningly sweet smile.

"Jess," Elizabeth said as soon as Suzanne was out of earshot, "maybe you'd better lay off a little bit. Don't you think you're coming on a little too strong?"

Jessica laughed. "Maybe," she admitted. "I'll

take it easy for a while. But I just can't resist getting off to a brilliant start."

"I feel sorry for her," Elizabeth said after a minute. "I don't know. I think maybe we're doing the wrong thing."

"Sucker," Jessica hissed. "Remember what happened last time, Elizabeth Wakefield! Are you going to let this girl walk all over you just because she's a good actress?"

"Well—"

"Trust me," Jessica sang out. "Just trust me, Liz. She can take it. I guarantee it!"

Elizabeth sighed. "I guess you're right," she said slowly. "But—"

"No buts," Jessica declared. "Come on, Liz. You've got to have a little backbone!"

"All right, all right," Elizabeth said. *I just wish it didn't make me feel so rotten*, she thought. But Jessica was right. She couldn't let herself be a sucker again. And Suzanne Devlin certainly knew how to take care of herself.

"Well, how do you think the Terrible Trio's doing so far?" Jessica asked. It was after dinner, and Steven, Elizabeth, and Jessica were stretched out in front of the TV set in the living room, watching a movie. The Wakefields were working in the den, and Suzanne had gone to bed right after dinner, claiming she was tired from the flight.

"Everything seems to be going just the way we planned," Steven said. "I think she's getting the idea."

"It's funny," Jessica said, rolling over on her stomach, "but I don't think she's all that gorgeous, Liz. I mean, she's pretty and everything, but she's way too pale. And I think she'd look better if she weren't quite so thin. Do you think she's anorexic?"

"No," Elizabeth said, "but she's definitely lost weight since she was here before. I asked her about it, in fact, and she looked embarrassed. She said she's been on some kind of new diet, but she doesn't want to lose anymore."

"Well, that explains it, I guess," Jessica said thoughtfully. "What do you think, Steve?"

Steven was quiet for a minute. "It's kind of hard to believe that she's still the monster she turned out to be last spring," he admitted. "To be honest, I was having a hard time *not* being nice to her. She seemed really great—very sweet, very interested in all of us."

"That's what makes it so hard," Elizabeth said sympathetically. "I feel the same way myself. *Maybe* she has changed."

"Hah!" Jessica snorted. "You thought she was great before she stole your necklace, before she tried to seduce Mr. Collins and then claim he attacked her. You've got to remember, this is no ordinary operator! Or *course* she seems nice and

90

charming! But that's what everyone thought last time, too. And look what happened!"

"Jess is right." Elizabeth sighed. "It kills me to look at Suzy now and think it's all an act. But she's just the way she was when she was here before—sweet, charming, willing to help. And last time it was all a big fake. So why should it be the real thing this time?"

"That doesn't explain why she came back," Steven pointed out. "The first time, maybe her parents roped her into doing an exchange, and she didn't want to come. Maybe she took some things out on people here. But this time she *begged* to come here. She gave up a trip to Saint-Moritz to come to Sweet Valley. Why would she get her kicks out of torturing people here? She could be rotten to the Swiss if that's all she's after. Maybe she really *does* want to apologize, to make up for her behavior."

Elizabeth shook her head. "It *is* confusing," she admitted. "We don't know for sure why she's here."

"Maybe her parents forced her again," Jessica pointed out. "Maybe they didn't want her with them. The food's really fattening in Europe." Jessica added. "If she really *is* neurotic about her weight, she may have come here so she could keep dieting. Maybe we should sneak butter into her food to make her gain weight. That would *really* torture her."

"How'd she get into her bed?" Elizabeth

demanded. "I thought you short-sheeted the bed."

"I did," Jessica said. "I spied on her, and she was remaking the whole thing. She looked completely baffled!"

"You're terrible, you two," Steven said suddenly, looking upset. "I don't think I want to gang up on the poor girl anymore. I've had enough!"

"Enough!" Jessica shrieked. "We've barely done *anything* yet."

"Still," Steven said, "I think we should leave her alone and give her a chance."

Jessica sighed. "Softies," she declared. "A whole family of softies. OK, you guys, just wait till she turns into Devilish Devlin again. Don't come running to *me* for help."

Elizabeth bit her lip. Was Jessica right? Or had Suzanne really changed? It was so hard to tell. But Elizabeth couldn't help siding with her brother. They'd been terribly unfair to Suzanne. And Elizabeth, for one, was prepared to be a little nicer to her the following morning.

But Elizabeth was only half listening to the argument between Jessica and Steve. The next day Todd would be there. And he was supposed to call any minute and tell her what time he'd be coming over.

When the phone rang, Elizabeth immediately jumped up, "I'll get it!" she said, practically running over Steven as she raced out of the living room to pick up the extension in the kitchen.

It was Todd, as she'd known it would be. All at once Elizabeth realized that Todd didn't know Suzanne was in Sweet Valley. "You're not going to believe it," she said into the phone when he asked her how everything was. "Guess who turned up at our house today?"

When Todd couldn't guess, Elizabeth told him. And from the shocked response on the other end, she guessed he was even more surprised than she'd expected.

# Seven

"Wait a minute," Todd said, clearing his throat. "You'd better back up, Liz. What in the world is Suzanne Devlin doing back in Sweet Valley?"

"We don't know, really," Elizabeth admitted. "I mean, we know what she's doing here—she's come to visit us for the next two weeks. But we really aren't sure what her motivation is for coming back."

"Hmm," Todd said. Elizabeth thought he sounded a little strange.

"You're upset, aren't you?" she asked. "I know it's kind of a pain, but so far I haven't seen anything that makes me think she'll really be in the way. She's acting awfully quiet—almost withdrawn."

"I'm not upset," Todd said. "I guess I'm just a

little surprised. Somehow I had the impression that Suzanne wouldn't exactly be welcome at your house again, after what happened last time."

Elizabeth sighed. Todd had been through the whole thing, too. As a matter of fact, he had been disgusted by what Suzanne had done. He said later that Suzanne was the sort of girl he couldn't stand—selfish, spoiled, completely sure she could hurt whomever she wanted and get away with it.

"I know. It's a long story. I'll tell you when you get here." Elizabeth lowered her voice.

"I've got an early flight," Todd told her. "It looks like I should be in Sweet Valley around ten or ten-thirty, since it's three hours earlier out there. And I'll come by the minute I've dropped my stuff off at Ken's!"

"Todd," Elizabeth said slowly, "are you sure you don't mind that I'm not coming out to the airport? Because if you want me to, I'll—"

"No, I like what you said before," Todd said. "About getting to be alone together right away this way. It would be too awful having to say hello to you in front of the Matthewses after so long!"

"Good," Elizabeth said softly. "Todd—"

"What is it?" Todd asked huskily.

"I just wanted to ask you—"

Elizabeth could hear the crackle of long distance between them on the line. "Oh, never mind," she said quickly. "I love you, Todd."

"I love you, too," Todd whispered. "And I can't wait to see you tomorrow, Liz. I'm going to hug you so hard . . ."

"Have a safe flight," Elizabeth said at last, hating to hang up, even with their reunion so close. "I'll see you tomorrow morning!"

"Good night," Todd said softly, waiting for her echoing "good night" before he lay the receiver back on the phone.


"Suzanne Devlin," Todd said aloud, shifting his weight on the stool next to the phone in his parents' brand-new kitchen. He could see the snow falling softly through the greenhouse window in the breakfast room. It still startled Todd to see so much whiteness. It was like magic, he thought, looking at the filmy glow through the flakes. Winter magic.

He sighed and turned away from the window. He ran through the conversation he had just had with Elizabeth, wondering why he hadn't told Elizabeth the truth the minute she'd mentioned Suzanne's name.

Todd had seen Suzanne Devlin recently. In fact, less than a month ago.

Todd had become a good skier since he'd moved out to Vermont with his family—not an expert, but good enough to enjoy a day on the big slopes without getting tired or aching the next day. The weather in Vermont was ideal for skiing. Already that year they'd had a record amount of snow, and he'd been out on the slopes most weekends since October.

A guy at school named Jerry Peterson was his favorite skiing companion. Jerry was a tall, well-built boy who was a forward on the basketball team at Lawrence High, Todd's new school in Burlington. Todd met him at basketball practice, and since then they'd become good friends. Jerry was relaxed and had a terrific sense of humor. He loved to ski.

Before long, Jerry knew all about Todd's life at Sweet Valley High. He'd seen Todd's collection of snapshots—with Elizabeth in almost every one of them—and he knew all about her and how much she meant to him.

Three or four weeks earlier, Jerry had convinced Todd to sign up for a school trip to Killington. Until then Todd had been skiing on smaller, less popular slopes. He'd heard of Killington and thought the trip sounded fun. "Who knows," Jerry had joked, rubbing his hands together, "maybe this will be my lucky weekend, and I'll meet some gorgeous ski-bunny in the Sugar Loaf lounge!"

Jerry didn't have a girlfriend, but Todd couldn't say that he wasn't looking. Wherever he and Todd went, he had his eye out for gorgeous girls. He always found a few, and he flirted quite a bit, but nothing much had come of it so far.

"But this time," Jerry had joked, "it'll be different."

And it was in Killington, at the very lounge Jerry had been joking about, that the two of them ran into Suzanne Devlin. It was about five-thirty in the evening, and Todd had just ordered hot chocolate at the bar. "Now, that's my idea of someone worth waiting around for," Jerry said in a low voice.

Todd followed his gaze, not certain at first who Jerry meant because the lounge was crowded. Finally he picked out a girl standing by the fire. She was wearing white flannel pants and a white sweater, but her back was turned and Todd couldn't see her face. "How can you tell?" he had asked. "You can't see her when her back is to you!"

"Believe me," Jerry said, "I can tell. Come on, follow me."

Todd was halfway across the room, trailing Jerry, when Suzanne turned around. He was so surprised he almost spilled his hot chocolate all over himself. "Wait a minute, Jerry!" he exclaimed, trying to stop his friend. "I *know* that girl!"

But it was too late. Jerry had already introduced himself, and Todd couldn't see any way out of joining them and saying hello.

*Jerry's right*, he thought to himself as he set

down his cup of hot chocolate. *Suzanne is still a knockout.*

"We've already met," Todd said brusquely when Jerry started to introduce them.

Suzanne, to Todd's surprise, looked glad to see him. She didn't look embarrassed, but when she took his hand, she smiled and added, "Under kind of crummy circumstances, I'm afraid. I'm glad I've gotten a chance to see you again."

It turned out that Suzanne was staying with her parents in a condominium in Killington for the weekend. "We come up fairly often from the city," she told Todd and Jerry. "Daddy's a marvelous skier, but I'm afraid my mother and I are pretty much useless."

"You haven't been out today?" Jerry asked, looking disappointed.

"No," Suzanne admitted. "I don't think I'd have the stamina. It's so *cold* outside!"

Todd gave Suzanne a second glance. It was funny, he thought, but he didn't remember her looking so frail when she was staying with Elizabeth. Had she lost weight, he wondered, or was he just imagining things?

"Why don't you join us for dinner?" Jerry said suddenly, looking hard at Suzanne. "I'm sure you and Todd have a lot to catch up on. We were just going to get a burger or something in town."

"Well . . ." Suzanne looked uncertain. "I can't

stay out very late. I want to get a good night's sleep. Can we be in by nine or nine-thirty?"

Nine or nine-thirty! Todd thought. Was this the sophisticated, big-city girl he had met in Sweet Valley?

Todd was certain his evening—and his weekend—would be ruined. But it was obvious that Jerry was crazy about Suzanne. And there was no time for Todd to warn him about what she was really like.

Half-an-hour later the three of them were sitting in a dark, cozy booth in a bustling hamburger restaurant. McMahon's. Suzanne would never put up with this place, Todd thought. It had to be way beneath the diplomat's daughter to eat in a place with a jukebox and sawdust on the floor.

But Suzanne looked delighted. After some confusion about who would sit where, she ended up sliding into the booth next to Todd. She smelled good, he found himself noticing. Not like the perfume she used to wear. No, now she smelled like soap and pine needles and fresh air . . .

Two hours later the three of them were still in the booth, laughing and talking. When the check arrived, Suzanne tried to snatch it out of Jerry's hand and bumped against Todd in the struggle. Her leg brushed his, and Todd's face turned bright red. "Sorry," Suzanne said lightly, starting to laugh again.

101

"Thank you both," she said when they dropped her off back at the lodge, "for a wonderful time. I mean it."

Jerry looked gloomy, and Todd could tell that his attempt to line up a date for the next afternoon had failed. "See you," he said, getting into his car again.

"Todd," Suzanne said suddenly, "I have to talk to you. Is there any way you could meet me back here tomorrow afternoon? Maybe we could take a walk or something."

"Well . . ." Todd thought fast. He didn't want to leave Jerry on his own.

"Please," Suzanne begged. "Todd, I really need to talk."

"How about two-thirty?" Todd suggested. That way, he thought, Jerry could get in some skiing before they drove back the following evening.

"Great," Suzanne said, her eyes shining.

"Way to go," Jerry muttered when Todd got back in the car. "What's your secret, Wilkins?"

"Come on, Jer," he said lightly. "She's a friend of Liz's. I met her in Sweet Valley ages ago."

"Who cares *how* you met her?" Jerry laughed, his bad mood lifting. "Look, pal, with a girl like that, it doesn't matter how. Just be thankful you did."

Todd laughed uncertainly. *I wonder what's up with Suzanne*, he thought. *She sure seemed different tonight . . .*

*       *       *

The next day Todd met Suzanne at the lodge, and they took a walk together as they'd planned. Suzanne looked even prettier than she had the night before. She was wearing a snow-white ski jacket with blue trim, and her cheeks were flushed from the cold. The two walked in silence for a while before Suzanne began to speak. She told him that her behavior at the Wakefields' house had been absolutely awful and that it made her sick to think about it now. "I was so angry with my parents," she recollected, her eyes misting over a little, "that I took it out on all of you. Anyway," she concluded, "I was over-joyed to see you last night in the lodge. I'd always hoped that we'd run into each other again. And I want you—if you can—to accept my apology."

For the next hour Todd and Suzanne contin-ued walking up a narrow trail, talking as easily and as naturally as though they'd been friends for years. Todd found himself noticing a number of things about her he'd previously missed—the dazzling effect of her smile, the way her eyes deepened to purple in the sun. *I like this girl*, he found himself thinking. *Really like her.*

Suzanne had stopped just then, turning on the narrow path to face Todd, her eyes afire with intensity. Todd's breath caught in his throat. She was only a few inches away from him. If he so

103

much as moved forward, touched her mouth with his . . .

Suzanne cleared her throat, and the moment was over.

"How's Liz?" she asked gently. "I've thought about her so much. Is she bearing up OK with you all the way out here?"

Todd heard himself begin to talk about Elizabeth—how busy she was, how much he missed her.

But he couldn't forget the way his heartbeat had quickened a minute before under the fir trees.

Had Suzanne felt it, too? Was that why she'd brought Elizabeth up?

For some reason, Todd felt unsteady as they walked back to the lodge. He could still remember it: the smell of the fir trees, the brilliant, blue-black sheen of Suzanne's hair against the glistening-white backdrop of snow. And the look in her eyes. Had she felt something too? Or was he going crazy?

Now, sitting in the snug, warm kitchen, Todd felt incredibly confused.

Why hadn't he just told Liz the truth? After all, nothing had happened, he reminded himself. By keeping it quiet, he was turning it into a bigger deal than it really was. But if he said anything now, she'd wonder why he hadn't mentioned it right away. He decided it was best to stay quiet about it. And when he had a chance, he'd tell Suzanne to stay quiet about it, too.

Because Todd didn't want to hurt Elizabeth—not for anything in the world. They'd looked forward to this reunion for months, and he wanted it to go perfectly, just the way they'd dreamed. Even though, he reminded himself, Suzanne was going to be there too.

It was beginning to look as if nothing was as simple as it had seemed a little while ago. In fact, Todd thought, it was beginning to look as if things might be getting pretty complicated that Christmas. And he had just helped to make things ten times more complicated than before!

"How can you possibly sleep?" Jessica demanded, sitting cross-legged on the carpet in Elizabeth's room, filing her nails with an emery board. "Do you realize how much we've got to get done before Christmas? It's crazy enough around here without having to work overtime making life miserable for Suzanne."

"Suzanne," Elizabeth pointed out, crawling into bed, "has been asleep for *hours*. Doesn't that mean we get to rest, too?"

Jessica frowned at her sister, gesturing wildly with the emery board. "Look," she said, "don't you realize tonight is the eve of one of the most important days of your life? *Todd* is coming tomorrow, Liz! How can you possibly just conk out?"

Elizabeth moaned. "With the lamp still on and all that noise you're making, I guess I can't," she mumbled, her face deep in the pillow.

"*I* can't sleep, either," Jessica said, "but that's because I've had nothing but chronic aggravation for the past few days. Do you realize," she demanded, flinging the emery board across the room, missing Elizabeth's dresser by a yard, "that Lila Fowler is at a spa right now? A spa!" Jessica made it sound as though Lila was committing murder even as she spoke.

"You're kidding," Elizabeth said, interested despite herself. "Where? Or, more to the point, should I say *why*?"

"She's toning her thighs," Jessica said, aggrieved. "For three hundred dollars a day. She's at some place called La Venue, where all the stars go when they've eaten too much over Thanksgiving and need to lose a quick five pounds."

"That's amazing," Elizabeth said, sitting straight up. "Three hundred dollars a *day*?"

Jessica nodded. "She left today—Cara told me. She'll be having massages and ultraviolet treatments and everything."

"Is all this just to get ready for the parade on Saturday?" Elizabeth asked.

Jessica giggled. "She's going to be livid when she has to get into that elf suit," she said. "But that's what she deserves. *I* would've won the title, fair and square. And I only used two little tea bags!"

"You could use the microwave oven," Elizabeth suggested, lying down again. "I'm not sure it's the same thing as ultraviolet, but . . ."

"Very funny," Jessica sniffed. "I don't care about any dumb old spa," she muttered. "I'm going to look a lot better than Lila does this Saturday, just wait and see. Besides"—she giggled—"no one will be able to see her glowing skin under all that green paint."

"Lila should find out Suzanne's secret," Elizabeth said thoughtfully. "She really is thinner. I wonder how she did it."

"Probably by being crafty, evil, and manipulative," Jessica retorted. "That'll make you lose weight any day."

Elizabeth was quiet. She didn't know what to think about Suzanne. She looked at her clock—it was after midnight. And she'd set the alarm for eight so she'd have plenty of time to get ready before Todd got there. Rolling over, she pushed her face into the cool pillow, and within minutes, she was sound asleep.

# Eight

Even after Elizabeth had finished her shower, Jessica was still asleep, curled up in a ball on the mattress on the floor, looking more angelic than Elizabeth could remember in ages. Elizabeth chuckled as she towel-dried her hair in front of the mirror. *Leave her*, she told herself. *Poor Suzanne deserves to have a problem-free breakfast.*

It was nine o'clock by the time Elizabeth went downstairs, and both her parents had already left for work. Suzanne was the only one in the kitchen. She obviously hadn't heard Elizabeth coming—she was standing over the sink, drinking a glass of water—because she jumped when Elizabeth came into the room.

"Good morning," Elizabeth said. "Did you sleep well?"

Suzanne spun around, her cheeks slightly flushed. "Uh—yes, thanks," she mumbled, slipping something into the pocket of her bathrobe. It looked like a bottle of pills, but Elizabeth couldn't tell for sure.

"Have you eaten?" Elizabeth asked, opening the Wakefields' pantry and surveying the cupboard shelves.

"I've just had some coffee, actually," Suzanne admitted. "I was about to get something to eat when you came in."

"Fine," Elizabeth said. "I'll get us both something if you'd like."

"Great!" Suzanne said warmly. "That'll give us a chance to catch up a little, too."

Elizabeth took a box of cereal out of the cupboard, wishing that the prospect of "catching up" with Suzanne was more appealing than it seemed. What was it that rankled so about Suzanne—her voice, her manner? She was so friendly, but Elizabeth couldn't listen to her without remembering everything that had happened the last time she came.

Suzanne seemed to be reading her thoughts. "I'm glad we're alone," she said in a low voice. "I've really been anxious to talk to you, Liz."

Elizabeth poured some cereal into two bowls. "Really?" she asked suspiciously.

Suzanne took a deep breath. "Liz—" she began.

"Strawberries?" Elizabeth asked her, taking a carton out of the refrigerator.

Suzanne nodded, looking as if she really hadn't heard the question. "Look, I know this must be dreadful for you three, having me come out here."

"Dreadful?" Elizabeth's eyebrows shot up. "Don't be silly," she said lightly. "Honestly, Suzy, we're happy you're here."

Suzanne flushed deeply. Elizabeth's tone was very different from her words, and it was obvious she wasn't sincere.

"Please," Suzanne begged. "Liz, I really want to talk to you. Don't shut me out!"

Elizabeth bit her lip. It was so hard, she thought. Anyone would think she was crazy not to trust Suzanne. She looked so earnest, and it looked as if she cared so much.

But that was how it looked before, she remembered. She couldn't imagine why this time would be different.

"Let's eat," Elizabeth said. "We can talk, too, Suzanne, if you really want to."

"I want to apologize to you," Suzanne persisted, taking a seat at the kitchen table. "I know I was a perfect beast when I was out here before, Liz. I was terrible to you. Taking your necklace—"

"It's nothing, Suzanne," Elizabeth interrupted. "Don't give it a second thought."

"And what happened with Mr. Collins,"

111

Suzanne continued, ignoring the blaze of indignation in Elizabeth's eyes. "I have a feeling that's the hardest of all to explain. Would you believe—"

"I'd believe anything," Elizabeth said coolly. "Would you like some milk for your cereal?"

Suzanne's lower lip trembled. "Maybe it would be better if I didn't talk about what happened," she began again. "But I feel—with you, anyway, Liz—that I've got to say something. I was going through a rotten time with my parents then, and I guess I was just kind of—"

"Rotten?" Jessica demanded, padding across the kitchen floor and yawning. "What are you two talking about?"

"Nothing," Elizabeth said flatly. "Nothing at all." She couldn't bear hearing Suzanne bring up Mr. Collins's name. When she thought of that horrible night, when she thought that he had almost lost his job . . .

Suzanne probably didn't know what it meant to need to work, she thought furiously. Maybe she thought Mr. Collins just taught for his own amusement. If he'd lost his job, what would have happened to him—and to poor little Teddy?

Mr. Collins may have forgiven Suzanne, but Elizabeth couldn't. No way.

"Suzanne," Jessica said sweetly, sinking down into the chair next to their guest, "I have to ask you something because I'm going out of my *mind* with worry. Have you seen the cream-colored silk blouse that was hanging in the front of my closet?"

Suzanne bit her lip, looking past Jessica to Elizabeth. "No," she answered. "Why?"

Jessica pouted. "Darn. I've looked *everywhere.* I bought it at Lisette's last week to wear to the dance at the Patmans' this Friday night. It cost a fortune, but I thought it was worth it because it really looks good, especially if I can get some sun before then. But it just isn't there! And unless someone just walked off with it—"

"I haven't seen it," Suzanne said quietly, taking a sip of orange juice.

Elizabeth glared at her sister. "It'll turn up," she said shortly.

"Things always do!" Jessica sang out sweetly, giving Suzanne a knowing look.

Jessica was really pushing it, Elizabeth thought.

"Tell me," Jessica continued, oozing fake curiosity as she turned her gaze on Suzanne, "aren't you absolutely bored to death here in Sweet Valley? It must seem like Dullsville after the wild life you lead in New York. Liz, did I ever tell you about all of Suzanne's *fabulous* friends? That one who—"

Elizabeth sighed. "Jess, do you want some cereal? I'm going to go upstairs and dry my hair."

"I'll get it," Jessica said, bouncing out of her

chair. "It'll give Suzanne and me a chance to get to know each other." She beamed.

"You really hate me, don't you?" Suzanne said in a low voice when Elizabeth had left the room. "Is it because of Pete? I had no idea he'd do something like that, Jessica. When Mother told me, I was absolutely—"

"I don't want to talk about Pete," Jessica said angrily. "It's none of my business, Suzy—but I really think your taste in guys is a little bizarre."

Suzanne sighed. "Jessica, it wasn't like that with Pete at first. I don't know why he pulled anything on you. He's obviously a complete jerk, and I'm sorry. He has trouble with his parents," she added thoughtfully, rubbing her forehead with her hand.

"I see," Jessica said shortly. "Of course," she added, "way out here in the sticks we don't see very much of that sort of thing. We find—"

"Way out here in *what* sticks?" Steven grumbled, coming into the room and pretending to get Jessica in a wrestling hold. Jessica tried to pull away as she heard the front door bell ring.

"Let me go!" Jessica wailed. "Steven, you're killing me!"

"Should I get the door?" Suzanne asked, getting to her feet.

"I'll get it," Jessica snapped, disentangling herself and racing for the front door.

"Well!" Steven said, giving Suzanne the first truly welcoming smile she'd had that morning

114

and grabbing an orange from the fruit bowl in the center of the table. "Did you get a good night's sleep, or did those two vampires keep you—"

"Daisies!" Jessica shrieked, hurrying back into the kitchen with an armful of flowers. "Can you believe it? My Secret Santa sent me daisies!"

"They're gorgeous," Suzanne said, her face lighting up at the sight of the blooms.

"Some Secret Santa," Steve said. "First a jewel box, now flowers . . ."

"I know who it is," Jessica said dreamily, imagining the look on Hans's face when he leaned forward to kiss her at midnight this Friday.

"Someone who really likes you, obviously," Suzanne said, smiling. "But what's a Secret Santa?"

Steven explained the custom to Suzanne while Jessica got a vase from the cupboard and began arranging the flowers.

"What a sweet idea," Suzanne said enthusiastically. "I'd like to have one of those myself."

Jessica snipped the bottom off one of the daisy stems. "You know," she said pointedly, staring straight at Suzanne as she spoke, "it never fails to surprise me when I get flowers. They're so incredibly beautiful, and they smell so wonderful. I always forget"—she snipped another stem—"that some flowers have thorns. Do you know what I mean, Suzy?"

Suzanne paled. "Uh—"

"Jessica!" Elizabeth called from the top of the stairs. "Could you come up here for a second? I need to talk to you."

"Excuse me," Jessica said sweetly, leaving the scissors and flower stems all over the counter as she hurried out of the room.

Suzanne stared after her, her face draining of color. Coming back to Sweet Valley was proving to be a great deal harder than she had anticipated. But she had vowed to stay and fight. And she wasn't going to quit now—however tough the battle seemed!

"Todd just called!" Elizabeth said, rummaging around desperately in her drawer for a sweater she'd planned to wear. "He'll be over any minute."

"Hey, did you tell Suzanne Todd was going to be in town?" Jessica asked suddenly.

"I forgot to," Elizabeth admitted. "Why?"

Jessica shook her head. "Just wondering."

"As long as Todd's had fair warning, I don't see why—" Elizabeth shook her head. "It isn't here. Jess, have you seen my light blue sweater?"

Jessica's eyes lit up. "No," she answered, "but I bet I know who has."

"Oh, come on, Jess," Elizabeth reproached her, spotting the sweater at the back of her

116

drawer. "Here it is. What do you think?" she asked critically, holding it up and glancing in the mirror.

"Pretty good," Jessica admitted. "Do you want to borrow my leather pants?"

Elizabeth laughed. "Todd would think I've changed too much. I better stick to these khakis."

"How do you think it's going?" Jessica wondered aloud. "Do you think old Devil-May-Care Devlin is getting the idea?"

"You're really making it pretty obvious." Elizabeth sighed. "Isn't there some way to be cool without being *icy*? I'm just afraid Mom and Dad are really going to be furious if they hear us carrying on the way we were just now at breakfast."

Jessica shrugged. "All the more reason to lay it on thick while they're at work. I'm sort of hoping she'll get the idea soon enough to leave before Friday night," she confided.

"Before Friday night! Are you kidding? We've got *weeks* more of Miss Devlin's company to endure! She just got here!"

"Liz," Jessica said reproachfully, "why do you think we're going to so much trouble? We're trying to get her to leave early, remember?"

"Jessica," Elizabeth said, surprised, "you don't really think she'll—"

"Give me a few more days," Jessica said calmly. "She's already so tense it's unbelievable.

117

A few more days and she'll be *begging* her parents to let her fly straight to Saint-Moritz. And that'll leave us the rest of the vacation, Devlin-free. We can have a wonderful time the minute she's gone!"

Elizabeth was thinking fast. "What do you think Mom and Dad would do if she asked to leave early? Wouldn't they be suspicious?"

Jessica shook her head. "Why should they be? They know how bizarre she is. Face it, Liz. It's the only way we'll be able to salvage the vacation. Suzanne's just too much of a pain."

"Well, I still think we could be a bit more subtle. I really don't want her to have a nervous breakdown or anything."

"Then you saw them, too," Jessica remarked.

"Saw what?"

"The *pills*," Jessica exploded. "What else? She must have a hundred and thirty-seven kinds of them in that little makeup case she's keeping under the sink in the bathroom. I tried to read the labels, but I didn't have time. Besides, all those things sound alike."

Elizabeth looked shocked. "You don't think she's really—"

"What, a pill-popper?" Jessica laughed. "Come on, Liz. What else is she doing with half a medicine chest in her makeup bag? That might explain the fact that she's lost weight, too," she pointed out.

Elizabeth nodded slowly. "You've got a point.

I *thought* I saw her with some pills this morning, but I wasn't sure."

Jessica sighed. "Trust me. What we have on our hands here is a hysterical, devious drug addict. And the sooner we get her out of here, the better."

"I think I'd better change really quickly," Elizabeth said suddenly. "Maybe we shouldn't leave her downstairs by herself!"


"Tell me more about what you have planned for this week," Suzanne said pleasantly to Steven. While Elizabeth had been dressing, Suzanne had changed into a denim skirt and a red silk shirt, and Elizabeth couldn't help admiring her as she and Jessica came into the living room.

"Well, there's the Christmas dance this Friday night," Steven volunteered. Jessica gave him a nasty look.

"Christmas dance?" Suzanne's face lit up. "Do you think I could come along?"

"Well, I don't—" Jessica began.

"Absolutely," Steve cut in, glaring at Jessica.

"I'd love the chance to see some of your friends again," Suzanne said, smiling warmly at Elizabeth. "Like Aaron Dallas, for example. I always felt terrible about—" Her eyes clouded over, and she shook her head slightly. "Anyway, I think it sounds terrific. I can't wait!"

"And there's the big parade on Saturday," Steven went on. "Jessica," he said, chuckling, "is going to be an elf. Isn't that right, Jess?"

"*Jessica*," his sister fumed, tight-lipped, "is going to be Miss Christmastime. Lila Fowler is going to be an elf!"

Suzanne gasped. "Miss Christmastime. That's wonderful! Did you win a contest?"

Jessica turned on Suzanne, her eyes darkening. "*No*," she seethed. "I spent the whole day wearing a garbage bag, as a matter of fact."

Suzanne looked horrified. "But—" The door bell rang but was muffled by Jessica's reaction.

"Never mind!" Jessica screamed. "Suzy, it's none of your business!"

Tears welled in Suzanne's lovely eyes. "I was only—"

"Quiet!" Elizabeth yelled, covering her ears. "Wasn't that the door bell?" she demanded, getting out of her seat.

"I'm coming with you," Jessica muttered, practically knocking her sister down in her haste to get out of the living room.

"Come on, Suzanne," the twins heard Steven say loudly. "Let's go in the kitchen and finish arranging Jessica's flowers."

"Todd!" Elizabeth exclaimed as she opened the door. She laughed as he engulfed her in a big bear hug.

It felt great to see him again. Elizabeth thought

120

he looked terrific in his tan chino pants and green sweater. The same old Todd—back at last!

Jessica was jumping up and down and hugging Todd, too. In fact for several minutes the three of them were a complete confusion of affectionate greetings and moist eyes. "God, does it ever feel good to be back here," Todd exclaimed, grabbing Elizabeth's hand and squeezing it tightly.

The next minute the twins heard a gasp from the hallway. Suzanne had come out of the kitchen, carrying the glass vase filled with daisies. But she stood frozen in the hallway, staring past the twins as if she were literally unable to move.

She was staring at Todd.

"Hey—it looks like I'm not the only out-of-towner around here," Todd said, trying to ease the tension.

Suzanne was still staring at him, her eyes clouding over and her arms trembling violently. And the next thing anyone knew, the crystal vase had dropped from her hands onto the floor in the front hall and broken into dozens of pieces. Water and daisies were everywhere, and Suzanne, trembling all over, burst into tears and rushed out of the hallway.

# Nine

"What was *that* all about?" Jessica demanded, staring down at the mess on the front-hall floor.

Elizabeth gasped. "Oh, Jess, your *flowers*."

"I'll go and see if she's OK," Steven said anxiously, hurrying into the living room after Suzanne.

"Let me help you," Elizabeth said to her sister, bending over to pick up a jagged piece of glass.

"I'll get some paper towels," Jessica said. "Be right back."

"Do I look horrible or something?" Todd asked Elizabeth, his brow wrinkling. "Or should I just get used to the fact that people drop vases when they see me?"

"Suzanne's a little tense," Elizabeth whispered. "It isn't your fault, Todd."

Jessica returned with the paper towels, and the three of them quickly cleaned up the floor. As they were finishing, Suzanne came out of the living room.

"I'm so sorry, Jessica," Suzanne said, taking a deep breath. Steven had his hand on her shoulder, but she was still trembling violently. "I don't know what got into me. I'm just really jumpy for some reason. Hi, Todd," she added, giving Todd a weak smile.

Jessica shot Suzanne a scrutinizing glance. "Maybe you'd better go lie down, Suzy. You look pale."

"I'm OK," Suzanne said, rubbing her temple with one hand. "I've just been getting these headaches lately, and they make me kind of dizzy."

Jessica raised her eyebrows at her twin. *Headaches?* she thought. *That's what happens when you swallow half a medicine cabinet with your coffee every morning.*

Elizabeth looked down in dismay at her chinos, which were soaking wet from the daisies she'd just carried into the kitchen. "Todd, I'm going to run upstairs and change," she said. "What time did you tell the Egberts we'd be over?"

"Any minute," Todd told her. "We'd better go as soon as you've got dry clothes on."

"I'm taking off," Steven said, "so I'd better say goodbye to you now, Todd." Steven was meeting some old friends for a football game and was already twenty minutes late. "Will you be back tonight?" he asked Todd, shaking his hand warmly.

"Sure," Todd said. "I want to say hello to your parents—and Liz and I have a date!"

Jessica followed her brother out to the garage, the rest of the broken glass in a garbage bag in her hands. "Steve," she said in a low, urgent voice.

"What is it?"

"What do you think's going on with Suzanne? Is it normal to get the shakes like that before lunch?"

Steven shook his head. "Lay off, Jess. The girl's got a right to be high-strung the way you're harassing her!"

Jessica glared at her brother, shoving the glass deep into the trash can in the garage and spinning on her heel. No matter what Steven thought, Jessica was convinced that something was definitely wrong. Suzanne just didn't seem normal. And Jessica was determined to find out exactly what was going on with Suzanne, once and for all!

When Steven and Jessica had gone out to the garage, Todd and Suzanne were left alone together in the front hall. "Come in the kitchen with me for a second," Todd whispered to

Suzanne, looking anxiously upstairs to try to judge from the sounds how close to being ready Elizabeth was.

Suzanne followed him into the kitchen, still trembling a little. "Todd, I'm so sorry," she whispered. "I had no idea you were coming to town! I guess—I don't know, I guess you just sort of surprised me," she concluded weakly.

"Listen, Suzanne," Todd said in a low voice, looking around him nervously, "I forgot to mention to Liz that you and I ran into each other in Killington. Somehow I just got sidetracked, and I'm afraid now it'll seem like . . ." His voice trailed off, and he stared at her helplessly.

"Do you want me to not mention it, too?" Suzanne asked.

"Maybe you'd better not." Todd sighed. "It's kind of dumb, but still—"

"Todd," Suzanne said sincerely, putting her hand on his arm and staring up at him with the sweetest, most serious expression he'd ever seen. "I'll do whatever you think is best. As it is, I've made such a mess of things . . ."

Jessica froze, her hand on the doorknob. She was standing just outside the half-open door, and she couldn't believe what she was seeing and hearing.

"Todd," she had distinctly heard Suzanne saying, "I'll do whatever you think is best. As it is, I've made . . ." Just then Steven started his

126

car and the rest of what Suzanne was saying was lost in the noise of the engine.

That little *rat!* Jessica thought furiously.

Everything had suddenly become perfectly clear to her. No wonder Suzanne was so tense. No wonder she'd dropped the vase. And no wonder she was so eager to come out to Sweet Valley when she could have been in Saint-Moritz, having the time of her life.

Suzanne Devlin was in love with Todd. And from the sound of it, Todd was hot on her, too.

Jessica shuddered, straining to hear more conversation between them. But the next minute she saw them walking out of the kitchen and then heard the cheerful sound of Elizabeth's voice in the entrance hall.

Trembling with rage, Jessica went into the kitchen. *That sneaky, conniving rat! First she stole my sister's necklace. Now she's trying to steal her boyfriend!*

Jessica couldn't help remembering Saturday night, when she'd asked Elizabeth what she'd do if Todd fell in love with another girl. Elizabeth had looked horrified. She might not have said as much, but Jessica knew the answer. *She'd die, that's what she'd do,* Jessica told herself.

"Oh, Liz," Jessica moaned aloud, her hand over her mouth. Imagine how her poor twin would react if she found out Todd had fallen in love with Suzanne!

Jessica had always suspected Todd might do a

low-down rotten thing like this. Sure, he seemed like a wonderful guy on the surface. But she'd suspected for a while now that he wasn't as great as he seemed. Still, she couldn't really put *all* the blame on Todd. No doubt Suzanne had gotten her hooks into him, and he'd gotten trapped. She could tell just by looking at Suzanne that she was an operator. The kind no guy could resist.

That didn't mean that Jessica forgave Todd. He didn't have the right to do *anything* behind Elizabeth's back!

But Suzanne was the one Jessica wanted to get back at. She was the one who had done her best to wreck the Christmas vacation so far. And now it looked as if she intended to make more of a mess of their lives than anyone had anticipated.

*Only*, Jessica vowed, *I'm not going to let her. If Suzanne thinks she can get Todd, she's got another thought coming. Because*, Jessica vowed to herself, grabbing the phone book and racing upstairs to her room, *I'm going to get her first!*


"What's up, Jess?" Winston asked, plopping down beside her on her striped beach towel.

"Yeah, what's with all the mystery?" Aaron demanded, stretching his own towel out beside hers. "You sounded like something really serious was going on over there this morning."

"It was," Jessica said grimly. "And still is."

It was two-thirty, the time the three of them

had agreed on for their emergency meeting at the beach. Jessica was killing two birds with one stone, using the strong rays of the sun to pick her tan up a little so she'd look more smashing than ever in her new blouse on Friday night. It had never really been misplaced after all. She'd just hidden it in the back of Elizabeth's closet to keep Suzanne on her toes.

"I can't thank you guys enough for coming to my rescue," she began, running a handful of sand through her fingers. "That girl is unbearable." She sighed. "Absolutely unbearable."

"What's she done now?" Winston asked sympathetically.

Jessica took a deep breath and began to list the atrocities Suzanne had committed since she'd arrived the day before. She was stretching the truth a little, but it was all for a good cause. "To begin with, I'm sure she's on drugs," Jessica said.

Aaron looked startled. "You're kidding! Really?"

"Positively," Jessica assured him. "She's even having dizzy spells now."

"Wow," Winston said. "What kind of drugs? Have you seen any?"

"Pills," Jessica told him. "All sizes and colors. She must carry about a hundred and thirty-seven pounds of them around all the time. And she looks really terrible, too. Liz says she's lost weight. I thought she was anorectic before I figured out that she's just high all the time."

"Incredible," Aaron said. "Well, what else? Has she been really rotten?"

"The worst," Jessica assured him. "You wouldn't believe how rude she is! She talks about Sweet Valley like it's some little hick town. All she can do is compare it to Manhattan. You'd think we all lived in one big *barn*, for God's sake."

Winston looked furious. "You see, Aaron. That's just what she said before—after we'd been so nice to her! I can't believe it."

Aaron looked thoughtful. "Anything else, Jess?"

Jessica thought fast. "I'm too embarrassed to tell you," she murmured.

"Come on!" Aaron begged her.

"I really shouldn't . . ." Jessica began, lowering her eyes. But one little fib, was nothing, she told herself, if it kept her twin's heart from being broken.

Just as she'd hoped, Aaron couldn't stand the suspense. "*Tell* me," he begged.

"Well . . ." Jessica sighed. "She said the guys out here were horrible. She said you were all really crass and that none of you knew *anything* about making a girl happy. And—"

"That's enough," Aaron said darkly. "I think I've heard just about as much as I can stomach."

"What can we do, Jess?" Winston demanded.

"I don't know about Aaron, but I'm willing to do anything you want—if you can think of a good way to get rid of her!"

"Nothing too drastic," Aaron warned. "All we really want to do is make her feel unwanted, right?"

"That's it!" Jessica said suddenly, snapping her fingers. "I just had a terrific idea! How would you two like to be Suzanne's Secret Santas?"

Winston's eyes lit up. "But instead of doing nice things, we'll do terrible things. Right?"

"Jessica Wakefield," Aaron said admiringly, "that's the best rotten plan I've heard in a long time."

"I thought you'd like it," Jessica said.

She didn't dare tell Aaron or Winston her suspicions about Suzanne and Todd. She'd never hurt Elizabeth like that. It would be all over town in a matter of minutes!

No, the subtle, underhanded way was far, far better.

This way, Jessica told herself, Suzanne was bound to get the idea that no one in Sweet Valley could stand having her around for another minute. And maybe then she'd get lost and leave Todd Wilkins to Elizabeth.

*All I can say*, Jessica told herself, *is that she'd better. Because Suzanne the Devil never knew what trouble was before!*

\*     \*     \*

Later that afternoon Jessica was lying on her stomach on a lounge chair by the pool, taking a nap. She was having a wonderful dream, too. In it she looked gorgeous. She had a drastic haircut, but it looked great on her. Hans was with her, telling her how beautiful she was. They were at the Patmans' house, dancing in the ballroom, but the other guests didn't seem to be around. Suddenly Lila Fowler appeared from nowhere, wearing an elf suit. She handed Jessica a silver crown. "You won, fair and square," Lila told her.

Jessica was just about to accept the crown from Lila and turn into Miss Christmastime when a horrible trickle of cold water began running down her back. "Stop it," she told Lila, who didn't seem to understand. The cold water became more insistent. "Cut it out," Jessica moaned, opening one eye. Steven was leaning over her, dripping water on her neck.

"Wake up, Sleeping Beauty," he sang. "It's time for you and me to make something wonderful for dinner tonight."

Jessica sat up, frowning. "I was *dreaming*," she said crossly.

"All the same," Steven said cheerfully, "it's almost five o'clock, and we have to think of something fabulous to make. Come on, my culinary partner," he crooned, grabbing her hand and pulling her to her feet. "Our pantry awaits you."

"Why can't Suzanne help you?" Jessica yawned. "I thought you two were on such good terms."

Steven laughed. "Just because I'm not trying to bite her head off every time she talks? Anyway, she's taking a nap."

"What do you think *I* was doing?" Jessica said, outraged. "Another nap?" she asked a second later. "What is it with these sophisticated city girls? She's barely been awake since she got here."

"I know," Steven said thoughtfully, shutting the glass door to the patio behind them as they went inside. "I'm sort of worried about her, actually."

"You're so gullible, Steve," Jessica complained. "You're much too nice for your own good. Can't you tell Suzanne's trying to fake us all out?"

"I'm not so sure. She got really dizzy when she was going upstairs, and if I hadn't caught her, she might have fallen and hurt herself. I think something's going on."

"You've been watching too many soap operas," Jessica said dismissively, padding into the kitchen. "Honestly, Steve, listen to your sister for once. That girl is poison. I'm convinced of it."

"Look," Steven said, "the world would end if you and Liz and I didn't have a major disagreement every once in a while. And this may be it! I think Suzy's OK. She was obviously terrible before, but she's admitted as much. Now she wants you to forgive her and give her a second chance."

"Hah!" Jessica snorted. She wanted to tell Steven about Suzanne and Todd, but it was obvious that he was on Suzanne's side. He wouldn't listen to anything negative about her.

So, if Steve wanted to be such a nice guy, she'd just have to let him. But she couldn't wait to see his face when he discovered what Suzanne was *really* like. Luckily Jessica had Aaron and Winston on her side.

Suzanne *said* she wanted a Secret Santa, Jessica thought, opening the refrigerator. And now she had two. Jessica was sure they'd bring her all sorts of surprises—the kinds of surprises that would make her incredibly homesick for New York. The kind, Jessica thought to herself, that would make her wish she had never set foot in Sweet Valley!

# Ten

It was twelve-thirty on Tuesday afternoon, and Elizabeth was famished. She had spent the whole morning at the Valley Mall with Jessica, and by lunchtime she was too tired—and too poor—to last much longer. Jessica had bought a bag of jelly beans, an oversize chocolate-chip cookie, and a pocket mirror to leave for Bruce Patman. Then she'd run into Cara in front of Kitchens 'n' Cookery and decided to help her choose something for her mother. "Go on home," Jessica had told Elizabeth. "Cara will take me back later on."

So Elizabeth had driven home alone. As she pulled into the driveway, she noticed that the mail had arrived. So, instead of going in the back way, she walked across the lawn, removed the mail from the box, then unlocked the front door.

"Phew," Elizabeth said, setting the Wakefields' mail down on the hall table along with her shopping bags. She'd done pretty well, actually. She found a record in Discount Discs that she knew Steven really wanted, and she'd managed to get away from Jessica long enough to buy her the scented body cream she'd been hinting about. A few silly gifts for Aaron Dallas had rounded off the list.

"That still leaves Todd," Elizabeth reminded herself, riffling absently through the mail. There was nothing for her, but there *was* something for Suzanne, a big red envelope. It didn't have a stamp on it, so Elizabeth figured that someone must have left it in the mailbox.

Probably a Christmas card from someone, Elizabeth thought, leaving all the mail in a pile and putting Suzanne's letter on top where she would see it. It had felt a little strange seeing Todd again, she thought as she carried the shopping bags up to her bedroom. They had gone to the Egberts' house after that strange scene with Suzanne—the latest in a series of scenes that were beginning to make Elizabeth worry about the girl. In fact, they'd talked about Suzanne all the way over to Winston's. Todd couldn't understand her behavior either. And he'd looked puzzled when Elizabeth told him that Jessica thought she was taking drugs.

"That doesn't seem very likely," he'd objected. "Maybe what Jessica saw was vitamins or something."

In the end they'd both started laughing, remembering what a disaster Suzanne's last visit had been. By that time they were at Winston's house, and any chance to have a *real* talk was out of the question.

They really hadn't been alone for more than a minute. Elizabeth thought she was imagining it at first, but she had a feeling that Todd was trying to avoid being alone with her—as if there was something he didn't want to face.

To begin with, he'd dragged her over to the Egberts'. Next he suggested they go back to Ken's house.

And the atmosphere there had been a little peculiar. That wasn't Todd's fault, Elizabeth reminded herself. Ken's house was filled with relatives, including his little cousins, who were jumping on Todd's or Elizabeth's lap and begging them to give piggyback rides. It had hardly been a romantic scene.

Still, Todd was a guest in Ken's home, and he said he felt he had to spend at least part of his first day relaxing with the family. Elizabeth had given up at about four o'clock, realizing they wouldn't get a chance to be alone together. "Tonight," Todd had promised her, "we're going to escape this madhouse and sneak off together—just the two of us. OK?"

OK? Elizabeth couldn't believe her ears. It was what she'd been waiting for! Finally they would have an opportunity to be by themselves so the magic between them could be rekindled.

What Todd had forgotten, though, Elizabeth thought, was the loyal affection of his old classmates. They weren't going to let his first night in town go unnoticed! "Ken asked us to meet him at the Beach Disco at nine o'clock," Todd told her when he picked her up. "I know, I know," he apologized, seeing the look on her face. "But he said he just wanted to buy me a soda. We'll take off after half an hour. I promise."

Elizabeth sighed. It wasn't Todd's fault that he was so popular. He couldn't help it that Ken had organized a surprise welcome-home party at the disco that would last until almost two in the morning!

And Elizabeth had to admit she'd had a good time. The Droids, Sweet Valley High's own rock band, had even written a song for Todd and Elizabeth! They played it for the first big dance number. It was called "I'll Wait For You"—and at least Elizabeth got to dance with Todd. Because that was the last time she saw him all night. Every time she managed to get near him, someone pounced on him, wanting to know all about Vermont.

"Kind of tough, having to share your romantic reunion with sixty other people," Jessica sympathized, breaking away from Hans long enough to join her sister on a bench at the edge of the crowded dance floor.

Elizabeth smiled. "I should have guessed Ken would do something like this," she said. "I *was* looking forward to an evening alone with Todd, but I'm glad he's having a chance to catch up with all his friends."

At last the party had broken up, and she and Todd had had some time alone together. Or almost alone.

"Liz, I hate to do this to you guys," Jessica said nervously, edging closer to her sister as the party was thinning out, "but it looks like Hans can't give me a ride home, so do you think . . ."

Elizabeth sighed. "Sure, Jess." Todd looked exhausted anyway, and she was so tired herself she could barely keep her head up. So they'd given Jessica a ride home, and their evening had ended with a hasty kiss on the Wakefields' front porch.

*Oh, well,* Elizabeth thought, taking out the Christmas presents she'd bought and wondering what to do about wrapping paper this year. *There's always tonight.* Todd was supposed to come over so he could spend a little time with Mr. and Mrs. Wakefield, who wanted to see him. Elizabeth and Todd had nothing planned— just a little TV, maybe a long walk. *And some peace and quiet!* Elizabeth thought. *A chance to see where we really stand . . .*

So far, she hadn't felt anything even *close* to

139

the old magic with Todd. But they hadn't had a chance, she reminded herself. She was sure the minute they got a few minutes alone together, it would be just the way it once was.

And this nagging little worry she'd been feeling for weeks would disappear.


"Suzanne, what is it? You look awful!" Elizabeth blurted out. She had gone downstairs to fix herself lunch, but the look on Suzanne's face made her forget everything.

Suzanne was holding the red envelope addressed to her in one hand, her face white as a sheet.

"Suzanne," Elizabeth repeated, "what is it?" But she might as well have been talking to a ghost. Suzanne was just staring at the sheet of paper in her other hand, her lower lip trembling and her face ashen.

"Liz," she said finally, her voice quavering. *"Look!"*

Elizabeth hurried over and scanned the piece of paper the girl had thrust out in her shaking hand. At once she could see why Suzanne was so upset. Someone had cut individual letters out of the newspaper, gluing them onto a piece of paper to look like a ransom note. "SUZY DEVLIN, GO HOME" the note said. "FROM YOUR SECRET SANTAS."

"I feel sick," Suzanne whispered, rubbing her

temple and pushing the piece of paper away. "Oh, Liz, how could anyone *do* such a rotten thing?"

Elizabeth's heart went out to the girl. "Come into the living room and sit down," she said gently. "I'm going to make us both a pot of tea, and we can have that talk you mentioned yesterday. How would that be?"

Tears welled in Suzanne's eyes. "I knew it was going to be hard," she whispered. "In fact, I thought maybe I was crazy to come back here. But I wanted to try. I wanted so badly to try."

A few minutes later Elizabeth had helped Suzanne to a cup of tea. The color was coming back to her face, and Elizabeth couldn't help being glad she'd been around to comfort the girl when she'd opened the letter. Suzanne had caused a lot of trouble the last time she was in Sweet Valley, Elizabeth thought, but that didn't justify this kind of cruelty.

"You see, I'm really serious," Suzanne told her sincerely, pushing her dark hair back with a slim hand as she lifted the cup to her lips. "I feel awful about what happened when I was out here before. I told you yesterday I don't have an explanation for it. I was going through a very difficult time—with Pete, with my parents. Especially with my parents." Suzanne grimaced as she set down her cup. "Liz, you wouldn't believe how jealous I was of you when I stayed here before."

"Jealous? Of me?" Elizabeth laughed. "Suzanne, how in the world could *you*—"

"I'm serious," Suzanne said quietly. "You see, I've always wanted to have a home like you guys do. Sure, my parents have money—tons of it." She laughed bitterly. "But time? Never. I got used to being lonely, or so I thought. But inside I always wanted . . . *this*," she said, gesturing around her. "A comfortable home. Parents who adore me, who want to be with me. A father who's more than just a signature on a check." She bit her lip. "Pete was bad news, too. My Mom was crazy about him because he had all the right credentials, if you know what I mean. His parents knew my parents. He had an expensive car and a lot of money. But he didn't care that much about me—not the real me, anyway."

Elizabeth was listening quietly, not saying a word. Something in Suzanne's expression told her that the girl wasn't lying. This time Suzanne was telling her the truth.

"Well," Suzanne said, staring down at her hands, "I just kind of flipped out when I came here before, I think. I didn't want to come, you know. My parents told me less than a week before I came that they'd arranged it. I never was given a choice."

"That's awful," Elizabeth burst out. "I never knew that!"

Suzanne shrugged. "That's the way my parents operate," she said softly. "*Used* to operate,"

142

she corrected herself. "A year ago they would never have heard of my not going with them to Saint-Moritz. But when I found out—"

"Found out what?" Elizabeth asked.

Suzanne's face paled. "Nothing," she said quickly, reaching for her mug again. Something in her eyes told Elizabeth not to press her.

She looked scared, Elizabeth thought. Scared and alone. Elizabeth wished there was some way she could reassure her—some way she could let her know that her secret, whatever it was, was safe with her.

"What I meant to say," Suzanne added swiftly, "is that we've gotten more honest with each other lately. I'm able to tell them how I feel, and they're much more willing to listen. So when I told them I wanted to come back here, they agreed."

Elizabeth didn't know what to say. "Suzanne," she began awkwardly, "I'm very sorry someone was stupid enough—and mean enough— to leave you that note. But you mustn't let it get to you if you really want to stay. It's one thing to make me understand, and I think I'm beginning to. But some of the other kids, maybe . . ."

"Liz, do you think I can do it?" Suzanne asked painfully. "Do you think if I really try I can make it up to some of them?"

"I don't know." Elizabeth sighed. "But I admire you for trying. And who knows . . ."

"I'm going to try even harder," Suzanne said

firmly. "Who cares about that stupid note? You know what I'm going to do as soon as I've made you a wonderful lunch?"

"What?" Elizabeth asked, taken aback by Suzanne's enthusiasm.

"I'm going to call Aaron Dallas and see if he'll let me take him out for lunch tomorrow," Suzanne said happily. "That seems like a good place to start, don't you think?"

"Sure," Elizabeth said, smiling at her. She didn't add that she doubted Aaron would agree to go. The poor girl had been through a hard enough time already. She would have to call Aaron Dallas and find out how angry he still was for herself.

"Hi!" Jessica called, putting down her shopping bags in the front hall. When no one answered, she walked through the house, opened the sliding door, and went out onto the patio. Sure enough, Elizabeth was by the pool, reading.

"How can you even bear to look at a book that size when we're on vacation?" Jessica demanded, dropping down on the grass next to her sister.

Elizabeth hurried to the end of the paragraph. "I happen to like reading," she said. "Did you buy me something spectacular for Christmas?"

"I bought you *something*." Jessica laughed. "Where's the Devil?"

"Taking a nap," Elizabeth said, rolling her eyes at her sister's nickname for Suzanne. "You know, it's kind of weird, Jess. I think she must be on some kind of medication that's making her sleepy."

"Drugs!" Jessica said. "I told you so. How come you never listen to me?"

"Not *that* kind of drugs," Elizabeth said. "I think she may be sick, Jess, really sick. She seems to get dizzy spells, and when she was watching TV earlier, she wasn't even looking at the set. I heard her tell Mom that she's having problems with her vision."

"Listen, Florence Nightingale," Jessica said, "forget Suzanne's drug-addiction side effects and tell me how things are with Todd."

Elizabeth laughed. "Well—"

"Wait a minute," Jessica interrupted. "I think that's the phone."

"I'll get it," Elizabeth said hastily, scrambling to her feet. "That's probably Todd now."

"Is Suzanne there?" a deep voice asked when Elizabeth answered the phone.

"No," Elizabeth said, trying to get her breath. "I mean she is, but I'm afraid she's sleeping right now. Can I take a message for her?"

"This is Aaron. Aaron Dallas. Who am I speaking to? Is this Jess?"

145

"Liz," Elizabeth told him. "What's up, Aaron?"

"I don't know. That's why I called *you*. I just got back to the house, and my sister said Suzanne left me a message to call her."

Elizabeth remembered now that Suzanne had tried to call Aaron after lunch. "Why don't you try again in a couple of hours?" she suggested. "I know she wanted to talk to you."

"Fine," Aaron said. Changing the subject, he asked Elizabeth if she'd had fun the previous night. After several minutes chatting with him, Elizabeth said goodbye and replaced the receiver on the hook.

"Well?" Jessica demanded when she came outside again.

"Well, what?" Elizabeth murmured, picking her book up and trying to find her place.

"Was that Todd?"

Elizabeth shook her head. "No, it wasn't," she said.

"Liz!" Jessica wailed. "You know I don't hold up well under torture. Who *was* it?"

"Aaron," Elizabeth replied calmly.

"Aaron!" Jessica gasped. "Well, why didn't you call me?"

"He didn't ask for you," Elizabeth said, turning another page and running her eyes over the words. "He asked for Suzanne."

"*Suzanne?*" Jessica looked as if she'd just swallowed something terrible. "What for? Did he say?"

"Jessica." Elizabeth set her book down in her lap. "For your information, I am *not* a switchboard operator. Or an answering machine."

Jessica looked hurt.

"Oh, all right," Elizabeth conceded. "I give in. He was calling back because Suzanne had called him earlier. She wants to take him out to lunch."

"She wants—" Jessica gave a short laugh. "Why? Is she going to poison him?"

"As a matter of fact, she wants to try to make up to Aaron after being so rotten to him the last time. And I think she really means well, Jess."

Jessica's mind was racing. "Yeah, I'll *bet* she does. Has Patsy heard about their little lunch date?"

"Jess, they haven't *made* a lunch date. And it wouldn't be a date, either," Elizabeth corrected her. "Suzanne just wants to be friends."

"Oh, Liz, you're so gullible. Suzanne doesn't want anything of the sort! She's obviously trying to go after Aaron, now that he's happily in love with Patsy. That would be just like her, wouldn't it?"

"You're wrong," Elizabeth said shortly. "That isn't what she wants at all. Quit jumping to conclusions, Jess, and give the girl a chance."

Jessica stared in disbelief at her twin. If she didn't love Elizabeth so much, she'd tell her what she'd overheard between Todd and

Suzanne the previous day. Maybe *that* would alert her sister to the fact that Suzanne was trying to steal every guy she could.

*But knowing Liz,* Jessica thought, *she'd probably laugh the whole thing off and say what I heard was nothing. That would be just like her. She'd tell me I'm making too much out of it.*

Well, Jessica had had it. She was sick of watching Suzanne's deceitful tricks being misunderstood by her entire family. Obviously it was up to Jessica to protect them all since they couldn't protect themselves.

And Aaron . . . jumping at the bait the minute it was offered!

No, it was clear to Jessica that she was going to have to do some planning of her own if she really wanted Suzanne out of the picture by Christmas day. If she could get Aaron to help her, and not wimp out as her own family had, it looked as if they'd have Suzanne exactly where they wanted her by Friday night.

*And exactly where we want her,* Jessica thought with a mean little smile, *is anywhere but Sweet Valley. And this time she won't come back!*

# Eleven

"Aaron? It's me, Jess," Jessica said twenty minutes later. She was in the study with the door closed so no one could hear her.

"Hi, Jess. What's up?"

"I'm calling about Suzanne," Jessica said pointedly. "Listen, Aaron, this is really getting out of hand. I mean, the girl is a complete lunatic!"

"What's she done now? I thought she was taking a nap. Liz said—"

"She *is* taking a nap," Jessica told him. "That isn't the bad part. She called you earlier today, right?"

"Yeah, that's why I called back," Aaron said patiently. "To see what—"

"Well, listen," Jessica said impatiently. "Do you know why she called?"

Aaron laughed. "If I knew why she called, why would I have bothered to call back? What is this, Jess, a cross-examination?"

"Aaron," Jessica hissed. "She's trying to *seduce* you!"

Aaron was quiet for a moment, then he said, "Jess, is this your idea of some kind of joke?"

"I'm dead serious," Jessica assured him. "Listen. Liz told me all about it, though she made me swear not to tell anyone. I guess Suzanne got all buddy-buddy with her this morning, and Liz pretended to go along with her so she could sort of find out what's happening, you know?"

"Yeah," Aaron said, sounding baffled. "I'm with you."

"Anyway, Suzanne told Liz that she wanted to take you out to lunch—some place sort of off the beaten track, you know? She said she wanted to get to know you better, if you see what I mean."

"Wow," Aaron said breathily. "And you really think she wanted—"

"I'm positive," Jessica said. "Believe me, Aaron, this is getting serious. We've got to do something before Patsy finds out and gets jealous!"

Jessica thought that little addition at the end was a stroke of genius. Patsy Webber was notorious for being jealous where Aaron was concerned. The slightest thing got her all worked up, and if she found out Suzanne was after Aaron, he could count on weeks of quarreling.

"OK," Aaron said. "What do we do?"

Jessica took a deep breath. "I've got a plan," she told him. "Do you want to hear it?"

Aaron sighed. "Shoot."

"First of all, call Suzanne back and act really friendly. Tell her you'd *love* to spend some time with her but you're too busy this week to make lunch. OK so far?"

"I guess so," Aaron said glumly.

"Good," Jessica went on. "Now, the next step is to set up Friday night. Suzanne's planning on going to the Christmas dance at Bruce's, but you've got to convince her that it's going to be terribly crowded and it'd be much more fun to go to a pre-party first. Can you make up someone who might have one—someone from college?"

"I guess so—my cousin Eddie," Aaron told her.

"Fine. So Eddie's having a pre-party and you want her to come. The problem is you can't pick her up, but don't tell her that now or she'll suspect something. Wait till Friday, about half an hour before the party's supposed to start, say around seven-thirty. Then call her up and say you have a flat tire, you can't pick her up, but you've got the address with you and can she meet you over there instead."

"Then what?" Aaron asked. "Where's she going to go? My cousin Eddie is married. He

151

doesn't want her driving over there. And I promised Patsy—''

Jessica sighed. ''Aaron, listen to me! Give her a fake address. Give her the address of the old house on Forrest Lane!'' She giggled. ''That's perfect!''

Jessica was referring to an old, dilapidated house on Forrest Lane, a lonely, wooded street on the outskirts of Sweet Valley. Everyone knew about the old house because some of the wilder kids used to have parties there before the police found out about it. Gradually it had gotten the reputation of being haunted.

''Wait a minute,'' Aaron interrupted. ''So I tell her to meet me at this great party on Forrest Lane. Then what do I do?''

''Nothing,'' Jessica explained. ''Just go to Bruce's with Patsy the way you planned! Suzanne will figure it out pretty quickly,'' she added. ''She's not *that* dense. She'll drive all the way out to this place, find it's just some old deserted house, and go back to Bruce's just like she planned from the beginning. Only,'' Jessica added, ''she'll realize what a jerk she was to believe you really wanted to spend time with her.''

''I don't know, Jess,'' Aaron said unhappily. ''It sounds kind of far out. What if she turns down the idea of going at all? Or what if—''

''You can handle her,'' Jessica said. ''Come on, Aaron. She's practically your *slave*. She'd die for the chance to get you alone!''

"That's another thing," Aaron pointed out. "The neighborhood up around Forrest Lane is awfully deserted, Jess. What if something happens to her? She could get hurt or something, and I'd—"

"Aaron," Jessica said patiently, "*nothing* is going to happen to her. She's simply going to turn around and drive back to Bruce's."

"Well . . ." Aaron hesitated.

"Listen," Jessica said, "if you don't want to help me, Aaron, it's up to you. I mean, it's *you* I was really thinking of—you and Patsy, I mean. You know Suzanne as well as I do, and if you aren't worried that—"

Aaron sighed. "OK, OK. I'll call her."

"Aaron," Jessica said happily, "I knew I could count on you."

"I just hope nothing bad happens to her. Because if—"

"Aaron," Jessica said sweetly, "don't you worry about a thing. The only bad thing that's going to happen to Suzanne is that she's going to get a little of her own back. She's going to realize she can't just stomp back in here and do whatever she pleases!"

"Here, here!" Aaron laughed. "Jessica, you should go into politics. You're really good at getting people on your side, you know that?"

*What a wonderful way to put it*, Jessica thought. Aaron Dallas was smarter than she'd realized.

"Oh, Aaron," she added suddenly, a thought

occurring to her. "When you talk to Suzanne, tell her not to mention anything to Liz, OK?"

"Why?" Aaron asked.

"Oh, you know," Jessica said vaguely. "Liz is funny about things like this. Just tell Suzanne that Liz wasn't invited to Eddie's and you're trying to keep it a secret so you won't hurt anyone. That should do the trick."

"Sure," Aaron said. "Whatever you say, Jess."

Jessica breathed a small sigh of relief. It was a good thing she had thought of that, she told herself. She didn't want her twin messing up the most perfect revenge scheme in the world!

Aaron Dallas's phone call, Suzanne reflected, as she sat in Jessica's room, was the first good thing that had happened to her since she'd arrived at the Wakefields'. Aaron had actually sounded pleased when she told him she wanted to take him out for lunch. "The thing is, there's no way I can make it this week," he had said regretfully. And he'd meant it, she was sure. He wasn't just making excuses. He really *wanted* to spend some time with her.

So Suzanne had jumped at the chance when Aaron suggested an alternative. "You're going to the Christmas dance at Bruce Patman's on Friday night, aren't you?" he'd asked her.

"Yes," Suzanne told him. "I'd planned to, anyway. Why?"

"My cousin Eddie is having a cocktail party from eight till ten on Friday. It's going to be a really small thing—just Eddie, his wife, and some of their friends from work. But I thought it might be nice if you wanted to come with me for a little while. Then we could head over to Bruce's. I don't think we'd miss much."

"I'd love that!" Suzanne had exclaimed. It was hard to keep the excitement out of her voice. A genuine invitation! Suzanne felt as if she'd won a major battle.

"I'll pick you up about seven-thirty, then, OK?" Aaron had asked.

"That's great," Suzanne told him, tears of happiness in her eyes. "Perfect."

"Oh, and Suzanne—don't mention this to Jessica or Liz, OK? It's such a small party I can't invite them, too. And I don't want to hurt their feelings."

"Of course not," Suzanne said warmly. "Well, that's great, Aaron. I'll see you Friday night."

Suzanne wasn't interested in Aaron romantically. He was simply a nice guy, someone she'd been cruel to the last time she was in Sweet Valley. She had heard he was going out with Patsy Webber, and she certainly didn't want to get in the way. All Suzanne cared about was that her suggestion had been met with kindness and enthusiasm. If she'd invited him to lunch and he'd turned her down, and sounded as chilly and unwelcoming as most people had so far . . . well, she probably would have given up. She would have called her parents and asked them if she could meet them in Saint-Moritz.

It had been a rough week. The one person who had surprised her the most was Todd Wilkins. After their meeting in Killington, she would have expected him to be a lot friendlier. She'd had fun with him that weekend. The day they had taken that walk together, she'd realized he was a wonderful person. So considerate, so mature for his age. And she had felt as though they had parted as friends that day.

Admittedly it had been a surprise to see him in Sweet Valley. But it was a pleasant surprise, and Suzanne had felt optimistic about the thought of having an ally the next week or two.

Instead, Todd had been particularly awkward around her since his warning not to tell Elizabeth about Killington. He barely looked at her when they were in the same room. When she asked him anything, he answered in clipped monosyllables. He seemed to want to keep his distance from her.

Suzanne shivered. It felt cold to her in Jessica's room, even though she had a sweater on and a blanket around her. Dr. Franklin had warned her about that. He said the medication couldn't help that. The blurring of her vision, maybe. And the terrible dizzy spells she'd been getting more and more frequently. But the chills wouldn't go away, no matter how many pills she took.

And neither would the fear.

No medicine in the world could help that. Suzanne sighed. Sometimes she wondered if she was doing the right thing keeping this a secret. Shouldn't she just tell them all?

But she'd promised herself she wouldn't. "I know it doesn't make sense," she'd told Mr. and Mrs. Wakefield, "but I want to win this battle on my own. I don't want anyone to pity me. If they knew—if the other kids knew . . ." She had shaken her head, her eyes filling with tears.

She'd had enough pity from her friends in New York. Out here, Suzanne had decided to fight this thing the hard way. And she was going to keep her secret, she told herself.

No matter what.


The twins were sitting in the living room with Todd and Suzanne, watching Mr. Wakefield adjusting the knobs on the television set.

"I made some popcorn," Mrs. Wakefield said, bringing in a bowl and passing it around. "Todd." She smiled. "I can't tell you how good it is to see you here again!"

But Elizabeth barely heard Todd's response. She couldn't keep this up, she was thinking. Something was definitely wrong, and she thought she should say something to Todd about it.

She didn't know whether it was her imagination, but he seemed so tense, so wound up. The way he was treating Suzanne, for example. It was embarrassing. He'd barely even said hello to her when he'd come into the house. And every time she spoke to him, he just mumbled in response.

It was one thing to remember that the girl was a pain before, she thought. But he was acting weird around her! The very least he could do was to be polite.

Elizabeth told herself things would ease up once the movie was on. But Todd continued to act strangely whenever Suzanne so much as looked in his direction.

"Am I in your way?" Suzanne asked from her position on the floor in front of the TV.

"What do you mean?" Todd asked, staring at her.

"*Todd*," Elizabeth said, poking him in the side. She couldn't tell whether he was trying to embarrass Suzanne or just wasn't paying attention. He seemed a thousand miles away. Once, when Suzanne asked him a direct question, he didn't answer. Another time, when she was minding her own business, he asked her to turn the volume up on the TV set and looked upset when she turned it down by mistake.

Elizabeth couldn't stand it any more. "Todd, let's take a walk," she whispered.

Todd was on his feet in a second. "Good idea," he said. He looked as though he wanted to be anywhere but right there.

"What's going on?" Elizabeth asked him mildly when they were outside.

Todd looked surprised. "What are you talking about?"

"I mean with you and Suzanne."

Todd stared at her. "What?"

"You're acting so weird around her," Elizabeth said impatiently. "I mean, it isn't as though you have to punish her single-handedly for what happened the last time she was here. She's been getting a hard enough time as it is. Jessica's driving her crazy."

"I didn't do anything," Todd muttered. "You're just overly sensitive, Liz. In fact," he added, "*you're* the one who's acting weird, if you ask me. You keep staring at me all the time with a critical look on your face."

"I do not!" Elizabeth said angrily.

"Liz," Todd said, grabbing her shoulders and turning her to face him, "what's happening? We haven't seen each other in months. And now we're arguing!"

Elizabeth dropped her gaze. "It's pretty silly, isn't it?"

"Do you know," Todd told her, "how many nights I've dreamed of walking this way with

159

you, of listening to the crickets, looking at the streetlights, and putting my arm around your shoulder . . ."

A lump formed in Elizabeth's throat. "I've dreamed about it, too," she admitted.

*But it isn't the way I dreamed it would be,* she thought unhappily. *Something doesn't seem right between us. I don't know what it is, but the magic isn't here anymore.*

"Todd, I'm so sorry," she began awkwardly. "I didn't mean to start an argument. I just felt so distant from you, so confused . . ."

"I know," Todd said huskily. "Liz—"

"What?" Elizabeth asked, searching his face for a clue to what he was feeling.

"Let's never argue again. OK?"

Elizabeth took a deep, quavering breath as Todd put his arm around her. "OK," she said finally, but there wasn't much conviction in her voice.

It wasn't until much later, when Elizabeth was tiptoeing across her bedroom, trying not to wake Jessica, that she realized Todd had never apologized for the way he was treating Suzanne. In fact, Elizabeth thought with a start, he hadn't said anything about it at all. That wasn't like Todd—not like the old Todd, anyway. Elizabeth was beginning to wonder if she hadn't been rash, promising never to argue with the new Todd again.

Because the new Todd, she thought uneasily,

never told her why he was being so strange around Suzanne. And the old Todd never would have acted that way at all, even if he had been provoked!

The old Todd. Elizabeth sighed. But where *was* the old Todd? And what could she do to bring him back?

# Twelve

It was Wednesday morning, and Jessica, Elizabeth, and Suzanne were on their way back from the grocery store. "What do you usually have for Christmas dinner, Suzy?" Elizabeth asked her, rummaging in the brown paper bags on the floor of the car to make sure they hadn't forgotten any of the things Mrs. Wakefield had asked them to get.

"We don't really have Christmas dinner," Suzanne said thoughtfully. "You see, for about ten years now, the tradition in our family has been to go on a vacation together for the week between Christmas and New Year's. It's nice," she added, "but it's even nicer being in a real home for the holiday."

Jessica sniffed. "I wouldn't mind spending a

Christmas vacation in Saint-Moritz," she remarked.

Suzanne laughed. "Yeah, Saint-Moritz is great. The strangest vacations were the ones we took when I was little. We used to go somewhere hot, like Aruba, or somewhere in Mexico. It was terrible! Can you imagine having piped-in Christmas carols playing while you're putting suntan lotion on in some resort somewhere?"

Jessica eyed her coldly in the rearview mirror. "Some of us," she said pointedly, "have *always* had warm Christmases. Isn't that right, Liz?"

Suzanne turned beet red. "Wow, I'm really tactful today," she muttered, hitting herself on the forehead.

Elizabeth grinned at her. Almost in spite of herself, she was beginning to like Suzanne. Once the girl relaxed, she had an excellent sense of humor and a natural vivacity that were appealing.

"Don't worry about Jess," she told Suzanne. "She's pretty thick-skinned. Aren't you, Jess?"

"Hey," Suzanne said suddenly, "do you think we could stop at the post office on the way home? I just remembered I've got a package from New York arriving there this morning."

Jessica swore under her breath, signaling as she moved into the left lane. "Now you tell me," she muttered.

"Jess," Elizabeth reproached her, "we're only about a block away from the post office!"

"A block in the wrong direction," Jessica pointed out, taking a right-hand turn so she could drive around the block.

"Sorry," Suzanne said. "I wish I'd thought of it earlier. I could've taken the car myself so you wouldn't have to go out of your way. Though I'm not much of a driver," she admitted. "In New York City, you can't get your license until you're eighteen. But I got mine—" she stopped herself. She had almost said "in Vermont," then realized that if she mentioned Vermont, Elizabeth might make some connection between her and Todd. "Out of state," she concluded vaguely. "But I haven't driven much."

"It's one of Jessica's greatest talents," Elizabeth teased. "Don't you think she'd make a great chauffeur?"

Jessica slammed on the brakes, scowling. "The post office, madame," she announced.

"Back in a flash," Suzanne promised, jumping out of the car and hurrying into the tiny building.

"What's with the special-delivery stuff, I wonder?" Jessica said impatiently. "This girl is so much trouble!"

"Actually I think she's OK," Elizabeth said lightly. "Don't you think you're being awfully hard on her?"

"What about Mr. Collins?" Jessica said. "What about the way she used you before? And Mom and Dad?"

Elizabeth was quiet for a minute. "I really think she's changed, Jess," she said finally.

Jessica shook her head. "Sometimes I just don't believe you, I don't understand how you can forget everything she did."

A few minutes later Suzanne came out of the post office, a tiny brown envelope in her hand. "That's the smallest package *I* ever saw," Jessica commented. "What's inside, jewelry?"

Suzanne didn't say anything, but Elizabeth thought her face looked almost pained as she struggled to control herself. "Nothing much," she said lightly, slipping the package into her blazer pocket. Her hand, Elizabeth noticed, was trembling violently.

Suzanne went right upstairs when they got home, "Leaving us to put the groceries away," Jessica commented. Another piece of mail from Suzanne's evil Secret Santa had been waiting for her in the mailbox, and a big gift-wrapped box with "Suzy" tagged on it was on the front porch. Only there was nothing inside. Suzanne was obviously upset and made some excuse to go upstairs.

"Jess, I want to talk to you," Elizabeth said quietly.

"I'm all ears!" Jessica said sweetly.

"Now, I've got to be fast because Suzanne's going to come down any second. But, Jess, I've been watching her very carefully, and I'm convinced there's something really wrong with her. I don't know what it is, but it all adds up. The fact that Mom and Dad let her come back here but wouldn't give us a good reason for it. The amount of rest she's been getting. And she's so frail looking! Plus all the pills . . ."

"It's an act, Liz."

"I'm serious," Elizabeth said, almost desperately. "Jess, believe me, I know what I'm talking about! Promise me you'll soften up on her. I'm really frightened!"

Jessica stared at her sister. Elizabeth really *did* sound frightened.

Was it possible she'd been wrong about Suzanne? Maybe the girl really did have something wrong with her. "OK," Jessica said seriously. "I'll lay off, Liz. If you really think there's something genuinely wrong with her . . ."

"I don't just think so," Elizabeth told her. "I'm convinced of it!" She folded up the empty brown paper bags and stashed them under the sink.

"Now, I'm supposed to meet Enid at the mall. After I help put these away, I mean," she added, looking with dismay at the groceries spread all over the counter. "Will you make sure Suzanne's all right while I'm gone?"

"Sure," Jessica said, a guilty flush spreading across her face. "I promise, Liz."

*I guess I'd better do some scheming in reverse*, she thought. *Because if Liz is right . . . if Suzanne came out here because she's sick and wants to make up with us all before she collapses or something . . .*

*Oh, God!* Jessica thought. *If that's really true, I'd better call Aaron as fast as I can and tell him and Winston to stop the nasty Santa routine! And I'd better tell Aaron to forget all about the fake party Friday night out on Forrest Lane.*

After Elizabeth left, Jessica went into the den to start wrapping Christmas presents. She was trying to decide how to wrap the bag of jelly beans she'd gotten Bruce when the phone rang. She picked up on the third ring, and Suzanne answered at the same time upstairs.

"Is Liz there?" Jessica heard a familiar voice inquire. It was Todd. Frozen, Jessica held the receiver to her ear but said nothing. *I should hang up,* she was thinking. *Suzanne may have some terrible disease, and it's none of my business what she says to Todd.*

"She's gone out shopping," Suzanne said, and paused for a minute. "Is this Todd?" Jessica heard her ask.

"Suzy?" Todd demanded. "Yeah, it's Todd." He sighed. "I'm glad I got you alone," he added after a minute.

*I'll bet,* Jessica thought, beginning to fume again. *I'll just bet!*

"Look, I'm really sorry I've been such a pain,"

168

he said awkwardly. "I mean, I know I've been really strange around you, but I guess I just—"

"I have to admit I've been sort of surprised," Suzanne told him. "I mean, after that day in Killington . . ."

Jessica completely forgot all thoughts of disease and compassion. *What* day in Killington? Elizabeth didn't know about this. Something was *definitely* going on here.

"I know," Todd said huskily. "Suzy, I know. When I asked you not to tell Liz about all that, I guess I didn't realize . . . I don't know. I just feel strange. I should have told her right from the start."

"Todd," Suzanne said gently, "don't blame yourself. You couldn't help what happened in Vermont! After all," she pointed out, "*I* was the one who asked you to come back to the lodge."

"I know," Todd said miserably. "I know."

"Look," Suzanne went on, "it would be silly to bring any of that up at this point! Anyway," she added, "Liz would understand."

*Don't bet on that*, Jessica fumed. She couldn't believe her ears. Todd had gone back to the *lodge* with Suzanne? This was much worse than she'd feared. Much, much worse.

"Well, I don't want to keep you on the phone," Todd said. "Maybe we can talk later. I'm sorry I've been such a jerk around you. And I promise to try—"

"Todd," Suzanne interrupted, sounding positively silky, "that afternoon we spent together was one of the best times I've had in years. But I never wanted to make things hard for you. Honestly."

"You haven't, Suzy." Todd sighed. "I'll see you later on, OK?"

Jessica listened to their goodbyes in a state of shock. She couldn't believe it. Her darkest fears had been right after all! Suzanne hadn't come out to Sweet Valley because she was sick. Nor had she come out to make up with anybody. She'd come because Todd was coming. That afternoon with him—that little tryst at the lodge—had been special enough for Suzanne to forget about Saint-Moritz and come racing out to the West Coast.

Jessica was practically shaking with rage. Suzanne had done it again—she had deceived them all, pretending to be so frail and so brokenhearted about her wrongdoings when all the while she was just waiting for Todd and flirting with him right in front of poor Elizabeth's eyes.

Jessica vowed to put a stop to it. She was not going to tell Aaron Dallas to leave Suzanne alone. If Suzanne thought she could steal Todd away from Elizabeth, she'd forgotten to count in Elizabeth's twin sister.

*Because* I'm *no sucker*, Jessica raged. *She can't make me believe whatever she wants me to. I know the truth. And I'm going to make sure she gets exactly what she deserves!*

170

*  *  *

In the end Elizabeth decided to buy Todd a scarf. "He'll need it all the way up in those freezing cold mountains!" she told Enid.

The two girls had stopped by Casey's Place for a cold drink before heading home. As always, Elizabeth felt immensely cheered, sitting across the table from her dearest friend. "One look at you, and my problems don't seem so insurmountable," Elizabeth told her warmly.

Enid giggled. "Thanks. Does that mean you look at me and think: God, I could look like *her?*"

Elizabeth laughed. "Not exactly. You're just a good shoulder to cry on."

"Why the tears? Isn't everything perfect now that Todd's back in town?"

Elizabeth sighed. "Enid," she said slowly, "this is kind of hard for me to admit, but I think some of the spark between Todd and me just isn't there anymore."

Enid stared at her, her green eyes wide. "You're kidding," she whispered.

Elizabeth shook her head. "It's strange. I mean, we're still very close. But it's a different kind of closeness. Don't get me wrong," she added quickly. "I still think he's incredibly cute and everything. But most of the time . . . I don't know. It just doesn't feel right. Something's missing," she concluded helplessly.

The waitress came over with their drinks, and

Enid thanked her politely. "Have you two talked about it yet?" she asked as she unwrapped her straw.

Elizabeth pulled her root beer closer to her. "Not yet," she admitted. "It's kind of hard, with all the chaos around our house. But I know we have to talk, and soon."

"It sure sounds that way," Enid said, shaking her head. "Boy, it's kind of hard to imagine you and Todd having problems. You always seemed like the dream couple to me."

Elizabeth sighed. "Well, I think in many ways we were unusually lucky. Everything always went our way, you know? But this move has been a big thing. It's made an enormous difference."

"Has he ever talked about other girls?" Enid asked.

Elizabeth looked taken aback. "No," she said. "It's funny, but I still have a hard time imagining that, though I guess it's just because I don't *want* to be able to imagine it. I'm sure he must have met girls he's attracted to, girls he would like to date. He wouldn't be normal otherwise!"

"How would you feel," Enid persisted, "if he told you that he'd met someone else? That he wanted to call things off because of another girl?"

Elizabeth thought very hard for a moment. "Enid," Elizabeth said carefully, weighing her words, "I'm not sure that Todd and I are going to be a twosome much longer. And if that's the case—as I'm afraid it is—I'd be delighted if he met another girl."

Enid shook her head. "Wow," she said. "You're really serious about this, huh?"

Elizabeth nodded. "I'll never forget Todd," she said softly, balling up the wrapper of her straw. "But I can't help feeling it's over now. Really over.

"And if that's the way it is, I guess I want Todd to make his peace with it, too. I want it to be mutual," she added. "And that's why I'm so scared to tell him how I feel. . . . Because, Enid, I'm afraid he won't want to let go. And if that happens, I don't know what I'll do!"

# Thirteen

Jessica was in high spirits Thursday afternoon as she prepared an early dinner. For one thing, she was excited about the Wakefields' plans to hear the *Messiah* at the civic center. Ordinarily Jessica hated classical music. But she loved Handel's *Messiah*. It was performed every year at this time by the Sweet Valley Choir, who dimmed the lights in the civic center and lit candles around them as they sang. It was so pretty that it gave Jessica chills. And it had been a Wakefield tradition for so long that it marked the *real* beginning of Christmas.

First they decorated the tree— an elaborate ceremony in itself, requiring a great deal of concentration and discussion. Mrs. Wakefield kept boxes of ornaments in the basement, and right after dinner the twins would race downstairs to get them. The endless giggling and playful fighting would begin as they tried to decide where each ornament would truly look best.

Steven had taken the twins out to Jason's Nursery that morning for the tree. And even though they said so every year, Jessica was positive this was the best one they'd ever had. It was almost eight feet tall and perfectly shaped, its blue-green needles filling the house with the festive smell of spruce. It was already set up in its customary place in the corner of the living room, just waiting for decorations—and piles of presents to be stacked beneath it.

But there was another reason for Jessica's good mood. Two more reasons. Lila Fowler was back from her visit to La Venue, and Jessica had run into her that day when she had stopped off at the mall to pick up something for her mother. Lila looked great. She was a little thinner, and her skin was positively glowing. Jessica would have been livid if she hadn't had a revenge plan worked out. The very thought of Lila in that elf suit on Saturday made Jessica want to burst out laughing.

And, on top of all that, Jessica had gotten another Secret Santa present—the best yet, as far as she was concerned. It was a menu from the Second Season, a new gourmet restaurant that had opened only a few weeks before. "Choose what you'd like now," Jessica read on the attached card. "This note entitles you to be my escort to this restaurant on the date of your choice—as long as the date of your choice is me. Love, your Secret Santa."

Jessica couldn't believe it. An intimate dinner at the Second Season with Hans! She was sure now he had to be her Secret Santa. Who else? Whoever it was obviously liked her—a lot. And he also had taste. Obviously it was someone refined, someone with a lot of class. It had to be Hans.

From what Jessica had heard, she had the best Secret Santa of any of her friends. Most of them were just getting the usual—a box of candy at the most, and more likely silly pranks. Like Olivia Davidson, having the swim team embarrass her to death with their rendition of "Silent Night." Jessica shuddered. Thank goodness no one had tried to pull that on *her*. The only person, she remembered grimly, whose Secret Santa even came *close* to hers was Lila Fowler's. Lila, she had to admit, was doing pretty well. But for the life of her, Jessica couldn't figure out who it could be. None of the guys knew—or none of them would tell her. Anyway, so far Lila had gotten real perfume, a *Vogue* magazine tied up with a ribbon on her doorstep, a gorgeous poinsettia—and the latest—almost as good as Jessica's invitation to the Second Season—a typewritten note promising a gourmet dinner for two prepared by her Secret Santa. Not as good as the Second Season,

Jessica thought, grinning. And Lila probably had someone terrible. Not like Hans . . .

Jessica hummed to herself as she opened a package of pasta. She was pleased with the dinner she was making. Red and green, she thought happily—spaghetti with tomato sauce and a big green salad!

Her good mood dampened a bit when Suzanne wandered into the kitchen. "That smells good," Suzanne murmured.

Jessica shrugged. "It's nothing much," she said curtly. Jessica couldn't even bear having Suzanne around since she'd overheard her on the phone with Todd. *That creep*, she fumed every time she remembered it. *Coming out here with her pretentions about wanting to make up, when Todd Wilkins is the only person around here she had the slightest interest in making up to!*

"Hey, did you make dinner?" Elizabeth asked, hurrying into the kitchen with a guilty look on her face. "Jess, I feel terrible. I've been downstairs, looking at some of the ornaments. Remember the ones we made when we were in first grade—those really horrible Styrofoam angels? Mom still has them!"

Listening to the twins' laughter, Suzanne felt a pang of loneliness. She had made a mistake, she told herself. She didn't belong out there. She should've gone to Switzerland.

Suzanne could imagine the scene at the hotel right now. Her father would be drinking a glass of scotch, and her mother would be giving him that warning look that meant, "You'd better take it easy on that stuff." They'd both be getting dressed for dinner. And getting dressed for the Devlins *really* meant getting dressed. A tuxedo and crisp white shirt for her father; some kind of glittery dress for her mother. Suzanne closed her eyes briefly, remembering the long line of successive Christmas Eves in hotels. It was always the same. Her parents went out somewhere, and Suzanne stayed behind. She hadn't minded very much for a long time. Every year there were other children in the same position, for the last few years in Saint-Moritz, the kids had made parties of their own.

But now . . . now Suzanne had something with which to compare those brittle, glamorous Christmas holidays. Looking around the Wakefields' cheerful, comfortable home, Suzanne felt her eyes filling up with tears. What she would have done to have a family like this—a home like this. To have a sister of her own age who shared everything with her—to have a mother who saved the ornaments she made in first grade . . .

"Suzy," Jessica said suddenly, giving her a strange look, "wouldn't you be more comfortable in the living room? I've got to drain the spaghetti, and I don't want to burn anyone."

Suzanne blinked. Jessica's message was loud and clear: *Get lost,* her turquoise eyes flashed. *Just get out of here and leave us alone.*

179

Suzanne was aware of how much Jessica hated having her around. And Jessica wasn't the only one. Whoever was sending her those stupid, cruel cards and empty presents clearly had the same message for her. *Go away!*

She would have done that if it hadn't been for Aaron's invitation. At least someone didn't want her to leave, Suzanne reminded herself as she walked slowly into the living room and collapsed into a soft chair. *Somebody* cared what happened to her. And as long as that was the case, she wasn't going anywhere—no matter how clear Jessica made it that she wished she would.

"Jess, that was a wonderful dinner," Mr. Wakefield said, leaning back in his chair. "And I wish we had time for second helpings. But it looks to me like we'd better get that tree decorated if we're going to make it to the civic center by nine o'clock."

"I'll do the dishes," Mrs. Wakefield said, getting up from the table. "Ned, you help Steve and the girls trim the tree."

"Mom, we can't do it without you!" Jessica wailed. She gave Suzanne a look out of the corner of her eye. "Maybe Suzanne . . ."

"I'd be glad to do the dishes," Suzanne said weakly, feeling embarrassed. "Go ahead, Mrs. Wakefield. I'll take care of everything."

Mrs. Wakefield laughed. "Absolutely not. I

wouldn't hear of it. Suzanne, when was the last time you helped decorate a Christmas tree?"

Suzanne blushed. "I don't think I ever have," she admitted.

"Just as I suspected." Mrs. Wakefield smiled. "You go on in there with the rest of them and see what it's all about. I'll join you in about three minutes."

Elizabeth felt a surge of affection for her family as she looked around the living room, strewn now with cardboard boxes. "Why don't we stick to just blue and silver ornaments this year?" Mr. Wakefield said hopefully, unwinding a strand of blue lights.

"Daddy," Jessica groaned, "*every* single year you say that, and we *always* end up with—"

Steven and Elizabeth burst out laughing. "A family joke," Elizabeth explained to Suzanne, who had just come into the room. "My father wants to have a tree like the ones he sees in *Architectural Digest*. And we can't stand the thought of wasting all our colored ornaments. In the end, Daddy always loses. We say, 'Oh, let's just add the *red* ones.' And then the *green* ones. And so on."

"OK, OK." Mr. Wakefield sighed. "I give up. Suzy," he said, "come over here and give us a hand."

Suzanne smiled and joined Mr. Wakefield by the tree. "You see," he explained to her, "these perfectly simple little blue lights are the first to go on. If it were up to *me*," he added with a grin, "the silver balls would go next, and that would be it. But the twins—"

"Dad," Steven exclaimed as he unwrapped an ornament from tissue paper that had yellowed with age, "I've never seen this ornament before. Do you know where we got it?"

A funny expression came over Mr. Wakefield's face as Steven held up a delicate glass angel. "Yes," he said softly. "That was my grandmother's. I had no idea that old ornament was still around. Let's put it up this year, OK?"

"It's beautiful, Daddy," Elizabeth said.

"Suzy, will you put it up for us?" Mr. Wakefield asked suddenly, turning to the dark-haired girl with a smile.

A visible shudder went through Suzanne's upper body. "No," she said quickly, "I can't—I mean, I'm not—" Her face turned ashen, and she grabbed onto the wall behind her as if to support herself. "I feel kind of dizzy," she murmured, staring down at the carpet. "I'm afraid I'd drop it or something."

Mr. Wakefield looked at Suzanne with sudden concern. "What is it?" he asked her. "Tell me exactly what feels wrong."

Suzanne's eyes fluttered a little as if she were trying to see straight before her but couldn't. Elizabeth's heart began to pound. She'd never seen anyone so pale before. "Daddy," Elizabeth said frantically, "what can we do? Is she—"

But Elizabeth's words were drowned by Jessica's scream. Suzanne had lost her steadying grip on the wall, and the next thing anyone knew, she had collapsed to the floor in a heap.

"I'm sorry, girls," Mr. Wakefield said when he came back downstairs, nodding at his wife in a way that clearly meant something to her, though it completely mystified the twins. "It looks like we're going to have to skip the *Messiah* this year. I know how you hate to miss it, but I don't want to leave Suzy alone."

"What is it, Daddy?" Elizabeth asked in a low voice. "What's wrong with her?"

Mr. Wakefield looked at his wife and shook his head. "She may just be tired," he said after a minute of silence. "She's been under unusual stress, and she seems very wound up. Other than that . . ."

*There's nothing wrong with her*, Jessica was thinking crossly. *Nothing but a little hysterical attention-getting!*

"But she fainted," Elizabeth persisted, "didn't she?"

"No," Mr. Wakefield said, "she didn't. She just slipped. She has . . ." He thought for a moment, and Elizabeth was convinced he was editing what he was saying, selecting certain things to tell them and holding the rest back. "She has a problem with muscular control, which is aggravated by stress. That's why she fell down. But she's fine now," he added, as if to reassure himself as much as the rest of the family.

A problem with muscular control, Elizabeth thought. What did that mean? Did it have anything to do with the pills she'd been taking?

"Look, Dad," Steven said suddenly. "Level with us. Is Suzanne sick or not? What's going on around here?"

Mr. Wakefield looked again at his wife. "Alice, do you want to pinch-hit for me?" he asked her. "I want to go upstairs and see how she's doing."

"You see," Mrs. Wakefield said when Mr. Wakefield had left the room, "your father and I are really in a tough spot. We promised Suzanne we wouldn't say a word to you three, and we haven't. And, to be fair to her, we can't—even now. I'm afraid if you want to know any more, you'll have to talk to her about it. That's the way she wanted it, and that's what your father and I agreed to respect."

Elizabeth bit her lip. *It must be serious*, she was thinking, or her mother and father wouldn't look so worried.

On the other hand, she thought, maybe it wasn't. Maybe Suzanne had a psychological problem like those patients she'd read about in social studies who got hysterical illnesses. Maybe that was why Suzanne was too embarrassed to tell them about it.

On the other side of the room, Jessica was reaching her own conclusion. It all sounded phony and farfetched, she decided, studying her mother's face and deciding she was just trying to keep Suzanne from looking foolish.

Obviously Suzanne had been too embarrassed to come back here without making up some kind of story, Jessica thought. She couldn't very well tell the Wakefields that she wanted Todd Wilkins! So what she told them was that she had some kind of strange, soap-opera type disease. And being the sweet, loving people they were, they'd bought it.

All Suzanne had to do was drop a few dishes and tell them she had "muscular control" problems. Muscular control! Frankly, Jessica could think of a few other kinds of control that girl was having problems with. And none of them had to do with dropping things or falling down.

One thing Jessica was sure of—Suzanne's theatrics weren't going to fool *her*. No way. She knew what Suzanne was up to, and she had a feeling all of this was supposed to make Todd feel sorry for her, too. Then, when he was convinced she wasn't long for this world, Suzanne would pounce on him.

And Elizabeth's heart would be broken.

*But I'm not going to let her get away with it*, Jessica thought angrily, remembering Aaron's fake "pre-party" the following night. Once Suzanne realized she'd been duped, that she wasn't the only one who could fake things around there, Jessica was sure she'd go away and leave them all alone.

Anyway, she wasn't worried about Suzanne. *Let the rest of them worry,* she thought. Jessica was sure that if anyone could take care of herself, it was Suzanne Devlin. And she didn't intend to waste a single minute worrying about her or her phony symptoms!

# Fourteen

Suzanne stepped back from the mirror in Jessica's room, setting her brush down on the dresser. "I wonder if I'm wearing the right thing," she said uncertainly.

Suzanne was too distracted about the night's party to realize she had never looked so beautiful in her entire life. The blue velvet dress she had borrowed from Elizabeth had a high neck, edged in cream-colored lace. It was much more subdued than anything Suzanne had ever owned, almost prim. But it looked amazingly good on her. It made her look like the heroine of a Victorian novel. A simple strand of pearls at her throat completed the look.

The blue fabric of the dress complemented Suzanne's enormous, blue-purple eyes. Her skin was as creamy and pale as the pearls around her neck. The only makeup she needed was a little blusher. A dab of perfume on each wrist and behind her ears, and she was ready. Or almost ready.

Picking up the package she'd gotten on Wednesday and opening it with fumbling fingers, Suzanne slipped out the vial of medicine inside. "That's strange," she said, shaking the envelope out and looking for the note Dr. Harrison always enclosed with a new prescription. That had been Suzanne's idea. She'd tried several different kinds of medication and was starting to get confused about what she could and couldn't do with each one. So she'd asked Dr. Harrison to be sure to include a list of precautions. But there was no note in the package. "I'd better call him." Suzanne checked her watch. It was seven o'clock. Aaron was coming in half an hour.

Still holding the pill bottle in her hand, Suzanne dialed the doctor's office, asking the operator to charge the phone call to her parents' number in New York. Several minutes later she was connected to Dr. Harrison's answering service. He'd already gone home. Of *course* he had gone home, she thought. It was ten o'clock in New York.

Suzanne studied the pill bottle carefully. "Darn," she said aloud. She searched through her shoulder bag and finally found Dr. Harrison's home phone number.

Again, she dialed the operator and charged the call. The phone rang four times. Then she heard the recorded message of an answering machine.

Well, it was practically Christmas. She couldn't expect Dr. Harrison to sit around, waiting in case one of his patients wanted to check in with him. Suzanne left her message and number on his machine. "I'm about to start the new medication you sent," she said, "but couldn't find any precautions in the packet. Could you call me back as soon as you can, please?"

The luminous numbers on Jessica's clock radio said 7:10. Suzanne sighed, shook a pill out of the container and headed for the bathroom for a glass of water. She didn't see why these pills should be any different from any of the others, she told herself. And anyway, she was all out of the last kind—not that they were doing a lot of good anyway.

Closing her eyes for a second, Suzanne popped a pill in her mouth, then took a big gulp of water to wash it down.

Cheers, she thought, tipping the glass at herself in the mirror. *Here's to my first victory—an honest to goodness invitation from someone who doesn't want me to get right on the first flight back to New York City!*

Turning the light out behind her, Suzanne slipped out of the bathroom and started down the steps. She could hear laughter from the living room, and she took a deep breath as she stepped down to meet Steven and the twins. The evening she'd been looking forward to all week was finally beginning.

*For once, she prayed, let everything be OK.*

Mr. and Mrs. Wakefield had gone next door to have a glass of wine with the Beckwiths, their neighbors, promising to be back in time to say goodbye before everyone left for Bruce Patmans'. Jessica couldn't believe her good luck. That meant they wouldn't be around to object when Suzanne took the car to "meet Aaron."

"You two look great tonight," Todd said, smiling at the twins. Elizabeth was struggling to get the cork out of a bottle of champagne the Wakefields had left for them.

"Thanks," Jessica said shortly. She could hardly bear to talk to Todd. But she had to admit that he was right. Elizabeth looked terrific in a shimmery, peach-colored dress with spaghetti straps. And she herself was wearing her new blouse with a pair of black satin pants.

Jessica had been planning this night for ages, and she wanted everything to go perfectly— right up until midnight, when the identities of the Secret Santas would be announced and Hans would come across the room, looking for her.

She pictured him taking her by the hand and pulling her in his arms . . .

"Todd," Elizabeth said, pushing the champagne bottle away, "do you think you can do any better with this?"

"Mom and Dad weren't kidding when they said to be careful with the cork." Jessica laughed. "They probably rigged it so we couldn't get it open!"

"Here," Todd said, struggling for a minute before a terrific *pop* signaled that the cork was out at last. "Quick!" Todd gasped as the bubbly wine began to stream over the top of the bottle. "Give me a glass, Jess!"

A minute later, as they were about to make a toast, Jessica said, "Wait. We're missing someone. Where's Suzanne?"

"Here I am," Suzanne said, standing in the entrance to the living room. Everyone turned to stare.

"Suzanne," Elizabeth gasped, "you look *gorgeous!*"

Steven, who had come into the living room just as the champagne was being poured, let out a long, low whistle. "You look fabulous," he said softly. "Absolutely fabulous."

But it was Todd's reaction that impressed Elizabeth the most. He turned a dull shade of red the minute he saw Suzanne, and the cheerful, relaxed expression on his face disappeared. He mumbled a greeting, barely meeting her gaze as Suzanne came forward.

"Have some champagne, Suzy," Elizabeth said, trying to cover up for Todd's rudeness.

Suzanne stared at the glass Elizabeth was extending. "I probably . . ." *Oh, why not*, she thought, taking the glass. She was sick of having to explain things all the time. Besides, Dr. Harrison had never said she shouldn't drink. He had said to limit it to a glass or two of wine.

Suzanne took a tentative sip. The champagne tasted delicious.

"I propose," Steven began, "a toast. Is everyone ready?"

"Ready!" the twins cried. Todd and Suzanne looked at each other, then both looked away. "Ready," they each mumbled, obviously embarrassed.

"OK," Steven said. "To a wonderful Christmas and a fabulous New Year. And may all of us find exactly what we're looking for—tonight and every night!"

"Cheers," Jessica said jubilantly, ringing her glass against his.

The phone rang, and everyone jumped. "I'll get it," Jessica said quickly.

Elizabeth was quiet, watching Todd. The two of them had not yet gotten a chance to have the talk Elizabeth had been thinking about all week. But something in Todd's behavior, especially in the way he looked at her, made her think he knew it was over between them, too. There was warmth in his gaze, yes. But no more magic.

"Suzanne!" Jessica called from the den. "It's for you!"

Suzanne carried her wineglass with her as she went to the phone. She hoped the call was from Dr. Harrison.

But it was Aaron Dallas. "Suzy," he said breathlessly, "is there any way you can borrow one of the Wakefields' cars?"

Suzanne's heart skipped a beat. "Why?" she asked. "What's wrong?"

"I've got a flat tire. The guy from the service station is looking at it right now, but it's going to take a little while. Anyway, I'm just about five blocks from the party and I thought I'd walk over. Can you borrow one of the Wakefields' cars and drive over and meet me?"

Suzanne looked anxious. "I'm not really that good a driver, Aaron. I'd rather—"

"Suzy, please," Aaron begged her. "Everyone's counting on you to come. I feel terrible, but there's no way I can come get you. I'll tell you what," he said quickly. "Let me give you directions. It's on a street called Forrest Lane. And if you can come, I'll be overjoyed. Have you got a pen?"

"Just a minute," Suzanne said, scrambling for one in the drawer of Mr. Wakefield's desk. "OK," she told him. "Go ahead."

"What do you think?" he asked her when he was done describing the route to Forrest Lane.

Suzanne thought for a minute. She took a big swallow of champagne, hoping it would relax her a little. "Aaron," she said, "let me see if I can get a car. If I can, I'll meet you at the party in twenty minutes."

"Sure, you can take the Fiat," Elizabeth said a minute later, "but I'm not sure I understand. You're doing *what*?"

Suzanne drained the rest of her glass of champagne, "I'm picking Aaron Dallas up," she said quickly, remembering what Aaron had told her about keeping his cousin's party a secret. "His car has a flat, and we'd agreed to go to Bruce's together."

"Go ahead," Jessica said, smiling at Suzanne with more warmth than she'd shown all week. "You're welcome to the car, Suzy."

"That's kind of weird," Elizabeth said as Suzanne went to the front closet in the foyer to get her coat. "Do you think Patsy knows that Aaron's taking Suzanne to the dance tonight? Why didn't she mention it before?"

"Good night," Suzanne called, picking up the car keys and heading for the garage through the kitchen. "See you guys later!"

Todd looked anxious. "You're right, Liz," he said, starting to pace a little as he thought about the situation. "Something's strange about the idea, though I'm not sure—"

"More champagne?" Jessica interrupted, holding out the bottle to refill Todd's glass.

She, of course, didn't see anything strange about it. And if finding an empty house didn't make clear to Suzanne how little anyone wanted her around, then Suzanne was crazier than she thought!

"We're home!" Mrs. Wakefield called, coming through the front door. "Are you still here?"

"Still here!" Jessica called.

Elizabeth didn't answer. She was staring at Todd, confused by his agitation over Suzanne.

Just then the phone rang. "Can one of you get that?" Mr. Wakefield asked, helping his wife take her coat off. Elizabeth set her glass down on its coaster and hurried into the study. As she picked up the phone, she noticed the note pad where Suzanne had been doodling when Aaron called: "1580 Forrest Lane," she had written down.

*I wonder what that is*, Elizabeth thought.

"My name is Dr. Harrison," the voice on the line said politely. "I'm trying to reach Suzanne Devlin. Is she there, please?"

Elizabeth blinked. "No, I'm afraid she isn't," she told him. "In fact, she just left a few minutes ago."

"Who is it, honey?" Mr. Wakefield asked, coming into the room.

Elizabeth covered the mouthpiece with her hand. "Dr. Harrison," she told him. "He wants to talk to Suzanne."

"I'll take it," Mr. Wakefield said, almost grabbing the receiver out of her hand.

"Where is she?" he demanded a minute or two later, hurrying into the living room. "Where did Suzy go?"

Jessica turned pale. "She—uh, borrowed the Fiat and went to pick up Aaron Dallas," she whispered, alarmed by the look on her father's face. "Why, Daddy? What's wrong?"

Mr. Wakefield's glance fell on the empty champagne bottle on the coffee table. "She didn't drink any of this, did she?" he asked urgently.

"A little bit," Elizabeth said, frightened. "Why, Daddy? What is it?"

"That was Suzanne's doctor," Mr. Wakefield said, obviously deeply agitated. "She left a message on his machine, and he was trying to get in touch with her. She wasn't supposed to have anything to drink. She's on very strong medication, and a glass of wine could completely knock her out—maybe even kill her!"

The color had drained from Jessica's face.

"I'll call Aaron," Elizabeth said, dashing for the phone.

"What time did she leave?" Mr. Wakefield demanded, grabbing his car keys.

"Daddy," Jessica moaned, tears filling her eyes, "Suzy didn't go to Aaron's. It was all a lie."

"What are you talking about?" Mr. Wakefield shouted. "Jessica, what in God's name is happening here? Suzanne's life may be at stake!"

Jessica burst into tears. "She's driving out to the haunted house on Forrest Lane," she sobbed. "Aaron and I tricked her. She thinks she's driving out there to meet him, but there won't be anyone there."

"Jessica, how could you *do* such a thing?" Mr. Wakefield demanded. "Never mind," he added shortly. "We've got to find her. With the combination of medication and alcohol in that girl's body, she'll be lucky if she makes it there alive!"

Suzanne blinked and leaned forward to swipe at the dashboard with her hand. It all looked so foggy—the window must be dirty, she thought, or were her eyes blurring again? She blinked hard and tried to concentrate on the road in front of her.

*Let me see*, she thought, trying to fight off the dizziness she was feeling. *Let me see. . . .* What had Aaron said she should do after Route One? She'd written it down somewhere, but where had she left the directions?

Suzanne reached into the pocket of her coat with one hand. The steering wheel was so slippery. It kept moving to the right, and she was so tired, so incredibly tired. . . . It was harder and harder for her to make out anything beyond the dashboard. It was all just a blur of shapes.

*I'm falling asleep,* Suzanne realized suddenly. *I'm falling asleep, and I can't . . . I can't . . .*

"Jesus!" the police officer in the squad car said to the officer next to him. They both stared in amazement at the red Fiat in front of them. "Someone's had a little too much pre-Christmas celebration already."

In shock the two officers watched the little sports car skid dangerously to the right, straighten out again, and suddenly bump off the road, turning over on its side.

The officer driving slammed on the brakes. He didn't know what condition the person at the wheel of that car had been in before. But he wasn't looking forward to seeing what condition the driver was in now.

# Fifteen

Elizabeth barely remembered how they'd all gotten in her father's car so quickly. Mrs. Wakefield was staying at the house in case they needed to telephone her. Elizabeth knew she'd never forget the look on her mother's face. She was white as a sheet, her eyes wide with terror.

And Todd—Todd was the one who was really scaring Elizabeth. He was trembling when they scrambled into the backseat along with Steven, letting Jessica get in front with her father. Although he was sitting next to Elizabeth, he seemed to be oblivious to her. He stared straight ahead, clenching and unclenching his fists.

"I think," Mr. Wakefield said grimly, backing his car out of the garage, "you'd better tell me how to get to this deserted house, Jessica. And then I'd like to hear your explanation of what is going on."

Jessica, her voice quavering, told her father how to get to Forrest Lane. "It's all my fault," she burst out as her father cut hard on the wheel. "If Suzanne's in trouble, if anything's happened to her . . ."

"Why'd you do it, Jess?" Todd asked savagely. "Why'd you try to hurt Suzanne?"

"Poor Suzanne," Jessica spat out, as if the words disgusted her. "Poor Suzanne . . ." She turned and glared angrily at Todd, but didn't finish her sentence. The next minute she burst into tears.

"OK, Jess, OK," Mr. Wakefield said. "Try not to get hysterical. I have a feeling we may all need to keep our wits about us. I just wanted to find out what happened. Why don't you start at the beginning, and tell us—"

"We don't even know where she is," Jessica wept. "Oh, Daddy, I feel so horrible!"

"Jessica," Steven began, "did this so-called party Suzanne was going to have anything to do with the other rotten things that have been happening to her? Like that letter she got telling her to go home? Or the crank phone call she got yesterday?"

Jessica blew her nose. "I couldn't help it," she said pathetically. "I thought she was deceiving all of you. I love you, and I couldn't stand seeing you made fools of. So I"—she gulped—"I was trying to protect you. And instead . . ."

"You didn't answer my question," Steven was pressing Jessica. "Come on, Jess. What've you been doing to the poor girl?"

"It wasn't just me," Jessica sniffed. "It was some kids at school, too—people she hurt when she was here before. It was all supposed to be silly," she added quickly. "Secret Santas in reverse—that was all! How was I supposed to know she was taking medicine? Or that she couldn't drink anything?"

"You couldn't have possibly known." Mr. Wakefield sighed as he turned off at the exit Jessica pointed out. "Your mother and I are to blame for that. Or in any case, we were involved in keeping Suzanne's illness a secret from you. That was Suzanne's doing, you understand. We wanted to let you know, but Suzanne was insistent. She wanted to try to make up with you without your pitying her." Mr. Wakefield laughed bitterly. "Her parents trusted us," he said. "And look what we've allowed to happen."

Nobody spoke for a minute. Elizabeth was too frightened to ask her father what kind of illness Suzanne had. It hardly seemed to matter. They had reached Forrest Lane, and the spotlights on her father's car picked out the desolate shapes around them—the old trees, the broken-down gates, the dead shrubs. At last they saw the turrets of the old house before them. It was dark and deserted, just as Jessica had described it.

Completely deserted. There was no sign of Suzanne—or the red Fiat—anywhere.

"OK," Mr. Wakefield said, making a U-turn, "I think we'd better get to the first gas station we can find and call the police."

"Daddy," Jessica said in a small voice, "what's wrong with Suzanne? Is she very sick?"

Mr. Wakefield was quiet for a minute. "Yes, Jessica," he said reluctantly. "I'm afraid she's a very sick young lady. She has a disease called multiple sclerosis, or M.S. as it's sometimes called, which attacks the central nervous system—and never goes away. She's very young to get something like that, but both her aunt and her grandmother died of the disease."

"What will happen to her?" Elizabeth asked, her mouth dry. "Isn't there a cure?"

Mr. Wakefield shook his head. "No. As far as what'll happen . . . it's hard to say. As I told you, Suzanne is very young to have this disease. The average patient who contracts it is closer to thirty or thirty-five years old. So her doctor doesn't know if she'll experience a decline at the typical rate or not. He's afraid—"

"Afraid of what?" Todd demanded, his face strangely pale. "What can Suzanne expect, Mr. Wakefield?"

"Typically," Mr. Wakefield said, "the prognosis is grim. M.S. is an incurable disease, though

Suzanne may go into remission and remain in remission for months, even years. Otherwise . . ."

"Go on," Jessica whispered.

"Otherwise, she may continue to suffer from attacks of dizziness and loss of vision. She'll be less and less able to control her muscle spasms and may have seizures. Eventually she'll be confined to a wheelchair."

"A wheelchair!" Elizabeth moaned. As hard as she tried, she couldn't imagine pretty, vivacious, independent Suzanne trapped in a wheelchair.

"And then what?" Todd choked out. "What happens next?"

Mr. Wakefield pulled into a filling station, turning off the car's motor. "M.S. is a fatal disease," he said quietly. "That's exactly what Suzanne didn't want you to know. She was afraid you'd feel pressured to forgive her. And she wanted you to forgive her anyway—because she doesn't know how much time she has left."

The silence in the car after Mr. Wakefield jumped out to call the police was deafening. Elizabeth felt as though her ears were roaring. She couldn't believe the words her father had just spoken. Yes, she'd suspected Suzanne was sick. But not this kind of sickness!

*Multiple sclerosis.* A shudder ran through Jessica. All of a sudden flashbacks from the past week flooded her mind: the phone call they'd made to New York when Liz tried to convince

Suzanne not to come; the horrible reception they'd given her; the moment Suzanne had dropped the crystal vase; the way she herself had pretended her blouse was missing, trying to make Suzanne think she was afraid it had been stolen; the way she had encouraged Aaron and Winston to pull rotten tricks on Suzanne . . .

Jessica felt sick. Really sick. She was trying to imagine what it must have felt like to be Suzanne this past week—to have dragged herself all the way out there, knowing the next time she saw any of these people, if she ever did, she might be in a wheelchair. A wheelchair!

Admiration for Suzanne welled up in her. She wanted to tell Elizabeth and Steven how sorry she was and how ashamed. But Jessica was afraid to say a word.

Every time she turned around, Todd's face silenced her. The look in his dark eyes . . .

Elizabeth had never seen Todd look like that before. But Jessica had.

Elizabeth and Todd had been in a bad accident together. Todd had bought a motorcycle, and he and Elizabeth had ridden on it together—just once. But a drunk driver ran them off the road that night, and Elizabeth was seriously injured. She was in a coma, and the doctors were afraid she'd never regain consciousness. Todd had had the same look on his face then.

He looked very frightened. As though the girl he loved was in terrible danger.

Jessica knew now that she'd only had half the story about Suzanne and Todd. Because Todd seemed to be in love with Suzanne. It was written all over his face. And no matter what Jessica did now to try to protect her sister, Elizabeth was going to find out.

"She's in the emergency room," Mr. Wakefield said briefly, jumping back in the car. "Let's go."

"What happened?" the twins demanded in unison.

"Is she badly hurt?" Steven asked.

"She went off the road on Route One about half an hour ago—maybe ten minutes after she left the house. A squad car was right behind her, the first piece of luck that poor girl has had in years. And they took her to the hospital in their car—they were afraid to wait for an ambulance. She's in bad shape," Mr. Wakefield concluded grimly. "They can't tell me what her chances are yet." He took a deep breath. "The Fiat flipped over. Suzanne suffered some pretty bad injuries, but the car's barely scratched." He laughed a short, bitter laugh.

The anger in Mr. Wakefield's laughter was the first thing Todd had responded to in almost an hour. He knew how Mr. Wakefield felt, he thought. As if fate had dealt Suzanne a horrible blow.

The news of Suzanne's illness had numbed Todd so much, he was barely aware of where he was. Elizabeth was next to him—he knew that. But all Todd could think of now was Suzanne. She had been on his mind just about every minute that week as it was. But now . . .

Todd hadn't admitted to himself how much he felt for Suzanne until Mr. Wakefield had put the phone down and said she shouldn't have had anything to drink. It was funny, Todd thought, but he'd sensed she was unwell. He just hadn't wanted to admit it to himself.

Nor had he wanted to admit what he was feeling when he saw Suzanne again. It was wonderful to be back in Sweet Valley, wonderful to see Elizabeth again. But it just didn't feel right between them anymore. He didn't know why, but that was how it was.

And he hadn't meant to act so strangely around poor Suzanne. The truth was, she'd made him uncomfortable because—because he was so attracted to her, he thought. A lump had formed in his throat. All he wanted now was to turn the clock back. If only he had admitted to himself what he was really feeling—and if only he'd been honest with Elizabeth. He could have arranged to spend this evening with Suzanne, and Jessica's stupid trick wouldn't have worked.

She'd still be sick, he knew, even if he had stepped in. He couldn't save her from that. But the car accident . . . Todd was convinced that was all his fault.

*And if she's still alive when we get to the hospital, I'm going to tell her so,* he vowed. *I'm going to tell her how I feel about her. And I've got to talk to Liz.*

Tears in his eyes, Todd inwardly willed Mr. Wakefield to hurry. He knew that even as they turned into the driveway of the Joshua Fowler Memorial Hospital, Suzanne was fighting to stay alive. And all Todd asked for now was a chance to tell her how he felt before the end.

# Sixteen

Mrs. Wakefield, pale and shaken, was waiting in the lobby of the hospital when the Wakefields burst in. "I already heard," she said, putting her hand on Mr. Wakefield's arm. "The police called me about twenty minutes ago."

"Have they told you anything about her condition?" Mr. Wakefield asked tersely.

Shaking her head, Mrs. Wakefield led them to the left elevator bank. "Dr. Ford asked us to go up to the waiting room on the second floor," she said. "He's trying to get in touch with her doctor in New York. On top of everything else, it looks like she may be going through complications from the new drug he gave her."

"What about the Devlins? Have you called them yet?" Mr. Wakefield asked.

"It's strange," Mrs. Wakefield said. "The hotel rang their room, but there was no answer. It's about six in the morning there, and maybe the phone just didn't wake them up. I didn't leave a message because I thought it might scare them too much. Oh, Ned," Mrs. Wakefield moaned, steadying herself against him, "if it were us, and Steven or one of the twins was in trouble and we were so far away . . ."

"I know," Mr. Wakefield murmured, stroking her hair. "Believe me, Alice, I've been thinking the same thing."

As they all got off the elevator, Mrs. Wakefield said, "I think I should try their hotel one more time."

"I'll come with you," Mr. Wakefield said, putting his arm around his wife. "Look, kids, do your Mom and me a favor and stick together in the waiting room, OK?" he asked. "The last thing we need tonight is for anything else to go wrong!"

"You can say that again," Todd muttered glumly, tracing the outline of a square of linoleum with his loafer.

"Poor Suzy," Jessica said, tears coming to her eyes again. "Do you think—do you think she'll pull through?"

Jessica's question hadn't been directed to anyone in particular, but Todd was the one who answered her. "Why would you care?" he said savagely. "Unless I've missed something, Jess, it seems to me that Suzanne's accident is all your fault!"

Elizabeth gasped, horrified. "Todd!"

"Look, guys," Steven said, trying to calm them all down. "We're all a little tense right now, and I think—"

"What about you, Todd Wilkins?" Jessica spat back. "Don't you think *you* have a little explaining to do, too? Maybe Suzanne's accident *is* my fault," she admitted, color burning her cheeks from a mixture of guilt and rage, "but what about her coming out here in the first place? Whose fault was *that?*"

"What are you talking about?" Todd demanded. "Jess, you aren't even making sense!"

"Killington," Jessica seethed. "Remember? That wonderful afternoon by the lodge?"

The color drained from Todd's face. "How— how did you find out about that?"

"What difference does that make?" Jessica retorted, tears spilling over. "The point is, you lured Suzy out here, Todd. If it weren't for you, she would be safe in Saint-Moritz with her mother and father!"

Elizabeth felt numb. It took her several moments to realize what Jessica was accusing Todd of.

Todd . . . and *Suzanne?*

Suddenly everything fell into place. The strange way in which Suzanne had reacted when

Todd arrived on Monday. The awkward way Todd treated her—as if he was afraid to let himself be nice. The way he avoided looking at Suzanne when she was in the room.

And his wild, almost crazed behavior tonight.

"Todd," Elizabeth said calmly, amazed by how clear her voice sounded, "did you and Suzanne meet each other again after her visit here? Before this week?"

Todd took a deep breath. "I wanted to tell you, Liz, but I was waiting for the right moment."

Jessica laughed hollowly. "Well," she told him, "this sure looks like it, doesn't it?"

"Jess, don't," Elizabeth begged her. Her head was beginning to throb. She couldn't stand this, she thought. She was so confused. How long had something been going on between Todd and Suzanne? Why hadn't he been honest about it?

"Liz," Todd said beseechingly, staring deep into her eyes, "nothing ever happened between Suzanne and me. Honest. I was skiing in Killington with a good friend of mine, and we bumped into Suzy in the lodge. At first I wanted to run in the other direction."

"But you resisted," Jessica said sarcastically.

"Jessica, *stop* it," Elizabeth snapped. "Let Todd finish!"

"My friend thought she was pretty," Todd continued, looking miserable. "He asked her to have a hamburger with us, and she said yes. So we spent some time together that evening, and I

212

thought she was different somehow—nicer. I didn't know anything about her being sick," he added, a pained expression crossing his face.

"That can't be the whole story," Jessica interrupted.

"I'm not through yet," Todd told her. "When we dropped her off at her parents' condominium, she asked me to meet her at the lodge the next day for an hour or two. She said she wanted to talk. So I did, and she told me she wanted to apologize for being—you know, being the way she was when she was out here last time. That was it," he concluded.

"You mean you never told her you were coming out here to visit?" Jessica asked.

Todd shook his head. "Why would I have done that? It was just a nice afternoon, nothing more."

"Then why didn't you mention it to me?" Elizabeth asked him. "Remember when I told you she was here? Why didn't you just tell me all this then?"

Todd bit his lip. "I don't know," he said softly. "I just felt weird about it. I know I should've mentioned it, but I just . . . I don't know why. I just didn't. And then I figured I'd better warn *her* not to mention anything either. Because I thought you'd be hurt, that you'd think it was a big deal precisely because I *didn't* mention it."

"And I thought you two had planned the whole thing," Jessica wailed. "I overheard you tell Suzy to keep quiet about something that happened in Killington, and I assumed—"

"Jess," Steven said suddenly, "is that why you've been trying to get back at Suzanne?"

Jessica nodded miserably. "I thought she was trying to steal Todd from Liz. I was afraid Liz's heart would be broken. So I was trying to get Suzanne to go back to New York before—"

"Shhh," Elizabeth warned. "Mom and Dad are coming back." *We'll have to continue this later*, she was thinking. Because there were still a lot of things Elizabeth wanted to find out from Todd, when they were alone together. He hadn't said anything about his feelings for Suzanne, but from the look on his face every time her name was mentioned, Elizabeth felt almost certain that Jessica wasn't entirely wrong about Todd and Suzanne. Todd clearly felt something for her, Elizabeth realized now.

But this was not the time to think about it. At the moment no one could tell whether poor Suzanne would be strong enough to live through the night.

"We got through to the Devlins," Mrs. Wakefield said, taking a seat next to the twins in the waiting room. "Those poor people—they're hysterical. God only knows what they must be feeling right now. They're going to do everything they can to fly out immediately."

214

"And we reached Suzanne's doctor in New York, too," Mr. Wakefield added. "He seems like a wonderful man. He'll be here on the first flight he can get."

"Have you heard any more about Suzy?" Jessica asked fearfully.

"We were about to ask you that." Mrs. Wakefield sighed. "No, we—"

"Mr. Wakefield?" a snowy-haired, kind-faced doctor inquired, swinging open the door to the waiting room and checking something on the clipboard in his hand. "Are you Mr. Wakefield?" he asked, reaching out his hand.

Mr. Wakefield shook it warmly. "You must be Dr. Ford," he said. "How is she?"

Elizabeth felt the tension as everyone silently waited for Dr. Ford to speak. Jessica was staring at the doctor's face, transfixed, as if she could will him to say something positive. Steven and Mrs. Wakefield were as white as paper. And Todd . . .

As long as she lived, Elizabeth thought miserably, she hoped she would never again have to see an expression like Todd's just then. All the anxiety, the misery, and the love were so plainly written on his face it hurt even to look at him.

"Well," Dr. Ford said, looking around at the stricken faces, "Suzanne is one lucky young lady. She's in stable condition. Frankly, considering the combination of alcohol and pills, and the car accident, I think it's a miracle. But she escaped with only minor cuts and bruises and a slight concussion."

The cries of excitement and jubilation that broke out almost knocked Dr. Ford off his feet.

"She's going to live!" Jessica screamed, throwing her arms around her mother.

"Hooray!" Steven hollered, picking Elizabeth up in the air.

"What can we do now?" Mrs. Wakefield asked.

"I would suggest," the doctor replied, "going home and getting a good night's sleep. That's what Suzanne will be doing, and right now there is nothing better for her than rest. Rest and time. Tomorrow morning, when Dr. Harrison is here, we'll start a complete round of tests."

Elizabeth felt almost dizzy with relief as she listened to the excited talk around her. But with the relief came a feeling of enormous confusion. From Todd's attitude toward Suzanne, she knew that he cared about her a great deal, perhaps more than he was willing to acknowledge. She herself felt surprised. And a little hurt. But not as devastated as she would have been, several months ago. She just knew that she and Todd had a great deal yet to sort out.

And now that Suzanne was out of danger, Elizabeth wanted a chance to see Todd alone, to find out exactly where—if anywhere—they stood.

*　　*　　*

"It's only eleven-fifteen," Jessica pointed out when they had all piled into Mr. Wakefield's car. "We can still make it over to Bruce's if we hurry!"

"Jess," Elizabeth groaned, "don't you think—"

"I want to go," Jessica said stubbornly. "I want to find out who my Secret Santa is."

"We could help Suzanne out if we went," Steven said thoughtfully.

"How's that?" Mr. Wakefield asked.

"Well, a lot of people around here still have the wrong idea about her," Steven said. "If we drop by the Patmans' we can spread the word about what happened and how rotten we feel about treating her the way we have."

"Steve's absolutely right," Jessica said, the pout on her face disappearing. "We *have* to go. It would be wonderful," she added, "if we could round up some kids to go over and visit her tomorrow, and—"

"Jess," Mr. Wakefield said, "no plans! I'll be happy to drop you kids off at the Patmans', and you're welcome to say whatever you please about Suzanne. But no one—I repeat, *no one*—is to make a single plan concerning that poor girl. She needs rest now, not one of your schemes."

"What are we going to do about the Fiat?" Jessica asked, suddenly remembering the car. "Where is it?"

"Jackson's Foreign Cars," her father told her.

"The police had it towed there. I'm afraid you kids will have to find some other way home. Can you get rides?"

"I'm sure we can," Jessica said blithely.

Elizabeth wasn't enthused about going to Bruce's, but she knew that Jessica and Steven were right about one thing. If they went, they could tell everyone what happened. It would mean the world to Suzanne if people forgave her. And even knowing how Todd felt, Elizabeth couldn't hold anything against Suzanne. She deserved some happiness—*real* happiness.

If Todd cared for Suzanne, Elizabeth thought, sighing deeply, she deserved Todd.

*And that's the very best way I can think of showing her that I think she's a wonderful person—someone I'd like to have as my friend.*


By the time the Wakefields and Todd arrived at the Patmans' mansion, the Christmas dance was in full swing. They could see candles shining in the ballroom on the second floor.

Bruce opened the door on their second ring. "Jess! Liz!" he cried. "Where have you been? We've all been frantic! Hi, Todd!" he cried warmly, slapping him on the shoulder. "Hi, Steve! Merry Christmas!"

Five minutes later they were upstairs in the ballroom, looking around with amazement.

"It's like being inside a Christmas tree,"

Elizabeth whispered. Suddenly she was glad they'd come. The room was entirely lit by candles, some gleaming in a chandelier and others on the tables that lined the room. At one end of the room stood the biggest tree she'd ever seen, gleaming with silver balls and blue lights. *Just like in* Architectural Digest, she thought, smiling. *Daddy would be happy*.

The Patmans had hired a live band, who were playing on a dais in one corner. And the dance floor was crowded with students from Sweet Valley High. Todd, Elizabeth, Jessica, and Steven were spotted as soon as they came in. Instantly they found themselves surrounded by friends, all wanting to know what happened.

"I'll tell you," Jessica said with a sigh, "since it was mostly my fault." And taking a deep breath, she launched into the whole story—everything, except the most important point of all. She didn't say a word about Suzanne and Todd.

"She's all right, your sister," Todd said a little later. He and Elizabeth were alone in the corner, listening to the music and sipping Christmas punch. "I'm sorry I blew up at her earlier. I was scared and didn't know how else to act."

"Todd . . ." Elizabeth began.

"Let me go first," Todd said. "Liz, I can't tell you how awful I feel about everything that happened tonight. I can't imagine how hurt you must be. If you only knew how much I care for you, how much I'll always care. . . ."

"Todd." Elizabeth smiled. "I could let you go on feeling guilty. But the truth is, I was getting ready to tell you that I thought we really weren't right for each other anymore—not as girlfriend and boyfriend. I've felt it all week. I love you," she added, "but I know that what we had is changing now into something else."

Todd's eyes shone with tears. "Liz," he said, "you are the most wonderful friend I've ever had."

"What you have to decide," Elizabeth said slowly, "is how you feel about Suzanne—and whether your feelings are affected by what you learned tonight about her health."

Todd shook his head. "It feels so strange, talking about another girl—to you!"

"I know," Elizabeth admitted. "I have to say I was a little stunned when Jessica dropped her bombshell tonight. For an hour or two there, I felt upset about it all. It's one thing," she said truthfully, "to have been having doubts about our relationship. But you and Suzanne . . ."

She shook her head. "The thing is, I've never really been the jealous type. You know that. And I want you to be happy, Todd, really happy."

"You're a pretty special person," Todd said huskily. "Liz, will you promise me something?"

"Sure," Elizabeth said. "What is it?"

"Wherever I am, wherever I go, can I always count on you to be my very best friend?"

Elizabeth smiled at him. The lump in her

throat had entirely melted. "Of course you can," she said, "though to be truthful, I know after a while, after you fall in love again, I may be edged out."

"Not on your life," Todd whispered. His eyes filled with tears as the band began playing the song he and Elizabeth had always considered "theirs."

"How about a dance," he suggested, "for old time's sake?"

"I'd love to," Elizabeth said warmly. And as Todd put his arms around her, she realized that she was OK. Really and truly OK.

It was practically Christmas Eve, and Suzanne was alive, and Elizabeth had her family and friends, who loved her. And she was dancing to a beautiful song with her best friend in the world.

Jessica couldn't believe it. *Winston Egbert!* Winston was her Secret Santa. The class clown had been the one sending her flowers, inviting her to the Second Season . . .

Even worse was watching Hans lead Lila Fowler out onto the floor. It just wasn't fair, Jessica thought miserably. Of all the rotten luck!

That meant, she reminded herself, that Lila would get a wonderful meal with Hans. And since Hans was living with a family, they would probably have the dinner at the Fowlers'. No one

221

else would be there, Lila would dim the lights—
*and I'll be at the Second Season with good old Winston
Egbert!*

She had to force herself to look interested
when the other Secret Santa pairs were revealed.
She danced with Bruce, who claimed the gifts
she'd left for him were just wonderful, though
Jessica was afraid they'd really been on the dull
side. Bill Chase, it turned out, was Olivia
Davidson's Secret Santa. It was his idea to have
the swim team serenade her.

Remembering that night at the Dairi Burger,
Jessica was suddenly seized by an inspiration.
Bruce was making a speech on the dais over a
microphone, and Jessica waited until he was
done before hurrying over to whisper in Mr. Collins's ear. He gave her a big smile and picked the
mike up.

"I know how much fun Secret Santa week has
been," he told the crowd, "and it's partly
because of that that I want to ask you all to think
about someone who didn't *have* a Secret Santa."

Mr. Collins went on to tell the entire crowd
what had happened to Suzanne. "She's in the
hospital," he concluded, "and I bet she'd sure
appreciate it if a few of you decided you wanted
to play Santa for her for the next day or two."

Mr. Collins's words were met with applause.

"Jessica," Elizabeth hissed, "didn't Dad
say—"

"This isn't a scheme," Jessica said innocently. "It's just a *suggestion!*"

Elizabeth smiled at her twin. "Merry Christmas, Jess," she whispered.

Jessica engulfed her twin in a bear hug. "Merry Christmas, Liz," she sang out.

"You know," Elizabeth said, linking arms with her sister as they looked around them to see whom they could ask for a ride home, "it's had some strange parts, but this Christmas hasn't really been that bad so far!"

"No," Jessica agreed, trying not to meet Winston's eye as he hurried toward them, car keys jangling in his hand, "it hasn't been bad at all!"

"Ladies," Winston said with a mock bow. "Rumor has it you are in distress and need a ride home. Could you *possibly* allow me . . ."

"You never know," Jessica whispered. "We've still got a while to New Year's, Liz. And it looks like it could get worse—fast!"

But Jessica was just kidding. And Elizabeth, hurrying over to tell Todd they had a ride, suddenly felt light as a feather. It was going to be a wonderful Christmas, she thought happily. And the beginning, she was almost positive, of the very best year yet!

# Seventeen

Elizabeth gasped. "I can't believe it. She did it, Todd, she really did it!"

It was Saturday afternoon, and Elizabeth, Todd, Enid, and several other of their classmates were watching the Christmas parade. Elizabeth couldn't believe that Jessica could really stick Lila with being an elf. But somehow she *had*. Because there was Jessica, wearing the silver crown and waving on the very first float.

And four floats back, a very grumpy-looking Lila Fowler was helping Santa pass out presents to the spectators. Lila was wearing a green trash bag just like the one Jessica had worn, and her face was covered with green paint. "She looks like a giant pea," Enid said, giggling.

Elizabeth laughed. It felt so good to have

things back to normal—or more or less back to normal, she reminded herself. Suzanne had made good progress overnight, according to Dr. Ford, but now that Dr. Harrison was in town, they were doing extensive tests to determine whether or not the new medication—and the concussion—had worsened her condition.

"You must feel pretty anxious," Elizabeth said to Todd.

"I do," he admitted, squinting at Santa's float. "I can't help wondering what's going to happen to Suzanne. You know, Liz," he added, "I have to admit that I don't even really know how she feels about me. Maybe—"

"Todd," Elizabeth said gently, "you'll just have to take your chances. Tell her how you feel!"

Todd would be OK, she thought. And she had a strong feeling that he and Suzanne would work things out.

As for herself, Elizabeth couldn't help feeling a twinge of excitement, wondering what the new year would hold in store for her. A tall, handsome stranger? she wondered, amused at how much like her twin she sounded.

In any case, she had no doubts about the breakup with Todd. They'd had a wonderful relationship, and Elizabeth knew she'd never forget him. But it was time for both of them to move on.

Deep inside Elizabeth found herself looking

forward to finding out what was waiting for her around the next corner. Maybe it would be a while before she found someone wonderful again. But Elizabeth knew that only time could take care of that for her. Just then, the future looked bright indeed.

"I don't know, Jess," Elizabeth said critically, wrinkling her nose as she surveyed the enlarged photograph from all sides. Jessica had propped it up against her bed for a "viewing session" before wrapping it.

"What do you mean, you don't know?" Jessica demanded, looking injured. "Can you tell me what in the world would make a better present for Mom and Dad?"

Actually, the photo had come out well. She and Jessica had linked arms, and their faces were turned slightly toward each other. "It's kind of scary how much alike we look," Elizabeth added.

"It's your luck," Jessica said sweetly, "to have a duplicate copy of *this* face." She dissolved into giggles. "Thank God Suzy's all right," she added a minute later, turning serious. "Liz, do you think she'll ever forgive me?"

"How could she help it?" Elizabeth sighed. "Hard as I try to stay mad at you, I always back down."

"What about Todd?" Jessica asked quietly. "Are you feeling OK about what's happening?"

Elizabeth nodded. "Todd and I have been far away from each other for a long time. Things were bound to change, and I just feel lucky that we'll still be friends. Honestly, Jess, I've sensed things were changing between us. So yes, I feel OK. Better than OK."

The telephone rang, and Elizabeth leaned over to grab it.

"It's Lila Fowler," Elizabeth said, covering the receiver with her hand. "And she sounds like she's having fits. Do you want to talk to her, or should I tell her you've moved to Mars?"

"I'd better talk to her," Jessica sighed and reached for the phone. "It's now or never!"

Lila was one person, she had a feeling, who was *not* going to find it hard to stay angry with her.

But every time she remembered how foolish Lila had looked in the elf suit, she wanted to crack up all over again.

It was worth it, Jessica decided. However angry Lila was, it was definitely worth it!

By the time the twins got to Room 312, it was almost seven o'clock. And they exchanged uneasy glances as they approached Suzanne's room, wondering what they'd find when they finally reached her side.

Elizabeth gasped when Jessica opened the door. The hospital room was crammed full of flowers and presents! One entire windowsill was lined with cards, and a baby spruce tree, fully decorated, had been set up in the corner of the room.

Suzanne was sitting up in bed, her black hair flowing over her shoulders. She looked pale, but more beautiful and radiant than ever before. And she was staring at Todd, who was sitting on the edge of her bed, holding her small hand tightly in his own.

"Excuse us," Jessica said, looking nervously at her twin to gauge her reaction.

"Suzy," Elizabeth said warmly, hurrying over to the bed so they would see at once she didn't mind. "I'm so glad you're all right!"

Suzanne blushed and dropped Todd's hand. "I'm more than OK, thanks to you two," she said. "You wouldn't believe this place. It's been like Grand Central Station in here! Bruce Patman brought the tree. And Winston and Aaron were here an hour ago. Winston brought me some crazy games, and Aaron invited me to have lunch with him."

"Suzy," Elizabeth began, shooting a look at Jessica. "I owe you an apology. I had no business treating you the way I did. If I've learned anything this week, it's that *everyone* deserves a second chance."

"I'm the one who really ought to apologize,"

Jessica chimed in. "Suzy, do you think you can forgive me for the horrible trick I pulled on you last night?"

"If you can forgive *me*," Suzanne said gravely, "then I'll be the happiest person in the world. That's all I want," she protested. "Jess, I don't blame you one little bit." Suzanne turned to Elizabeth. "Todd has explained a great deal to me, and I understand now why Jess did what she did. But the way I acted the first time I came out here . . . I really didn't have an excuse. That's why I need to beg you"—she hung her head—"to forgive me anyway."

The next minutes both twins were on the bed, hugging Suzanne and crying.

"What's going *on* in here?" Steven demanded, opening the door. "Never mind," he added, as if something had just occurred to him. "Tell me later. Mom, Dad, and two doctors are on their way in here, so you guys better look normal!"

At once the twins bounced off the bed, dragging Todd with them. Steven was right. The door opened a moment later.

Elizabeth knew something was up the minute she saw her mother's face. It was shining with joy.

"Suzanne," Dr. Ford said, "I hate to put you through a long medical talk, so I'm going to let Dr. Harrison take over for me and tell you himself what we found out today. But I think,"—his blue eyes twinkled—"that you'll agree with me that it's about the best Christmas present we could have hoped to give you."

Dr. Harrison, a spry, gray-haired man in his early sixties, came over and sat down on the bed where Todd had been a minute ago. "Suzy," he began, "remember when you first started coming in for tests and I asked you if you'd had a virus lately?"

Suzanne nodded. "I hadn't," she said. "That's why—"

Dr. Harrison held up his hand. "You did," he told her ruefully. "And that's where all the mistakes began."

"Mistakes?" Suzanne said. "But—"

"You had a very common virus—mononucleosis," Dr. Harrison told her. "Only it was an undetected case. Remember you complained of feeling tired and headachy for a month or two?"

Suzanne nodded. "Yes, but I still don't understand."

"Suzy," Dr. Harrison burst out, "you don't have multiple sclerosis at all! We've been racking our brains all day, and we finally figured out what happened. You see, you had an undetected virus and several months later began to experience a very rare complication from it."

Suzanne was staring at him, hanging onto his every word. "Go on," she whispered.

"This complication is an infection of the central nervous system," Dr. Harrison continued, "resulting in dizziness, blurring, and occasional

231

loss of muscle control. Suzanne, you never had M.S. I've been treating you for a disease that you don't have!"

Suzanne burst into tears. "You mean—" she said brokenly, clutching onto the doctor's arm, "you mean I'm normal, like everyone else?"

Elizabeth felt a lump forming in her throat. She felt as though she were seeing a miracle take place in front of her.

Across the room, she saw the look on Todd's face and guessed what he was feeling. *It's a new beginning for us all*, Elizabeth thought. *A new chance for all of us to find*—what were the words her brother had said when he was making his toast the night before?—*what we all want tonight, and every night*, Elizabeth thought.

The next thing anyone knew, the door to Suzy's room burst open. "Suzanne!" Mr. Devlin cried, rushing across the room to take his daughter in his arms.

Mrs. Devlin was right behind him. "I—I'm afraid I don't know who these people are," she said, gesturing toward the door.

"Liz!" Jessica gasped, clutching her arm.

It was the entire swim team, plus some of their friends, this time clad in shorts and T-shirts that were decorated with green letters. When the boys had fanned themselves out as best they could in the crowded room, the letters spelled "Merry Christmas, Suzy."

And the next thing Elizabeth knew, Bill Chase

had sounded a note on his harmonica, and the whole group burst into the first line of "Silent Night."

Elizabeth didn't know whether she wanted to laugh or cry. The swimmers looked insane with their arms around each other. But there was something warm and touching about their singing. She could tell how happy Suzanne was, too. She looked as if she was about to burst with joy.

"Merry Christmas, Liz," she heard Jessica whisper again.

But Elizabeth's heart was too full to answer. It certainly was, she thought happily. Everyone was together, safe and healthy and glad. Christmas had arrived at last!

# PUT YOURSELF IN THE PICTURE!

*Enter the SWEET DREAMS® Cover Girl Contest and see yourself on the cover of a SWEET DREAMS book!*

If you've ever dreamed of becoming a model and seeing your face gazing from the covers of books all across America, this is the contest for you!

Girls from age 11 to 16 are eligible. Just fill out the coupon below and send it in, along with two photographs of yourself (one close-up and one full length standing pose)* and an essay telling why you enjoy SWEET DREAMS books. The Grand Prize Winner will be chosen by an expert panel of judges—including a beauty editor from *Young Miss* magazine!

The Grand Prize is a trip to New York City for you and your chaperone, where you will be photographed for the cover of an upcoming SWEET DREAMS novel! The Grand Prize Winner will also receive a complete professional makeover, have an interview at a top modeling agency and enjoy a dinner date with a SWEET DREAMS author!

Five lucky Second Prize Winners will receive make-up kits!

So don't delay—enter the contest today!

*Photographs must have been taken within 6 months of contest entry.

SWEET DREAMS Cover Girl Contest
Bantam Books, Inc.
Dept. NP
666 Fifth Avenue
New York, NY 10103

Name_____Age_____

Address_____

City _____ State _____ Zip _____

Exp. 12/31/85

C17—9/85